THE REBEL WITHIN

Charli Gargett

Contents

1. Chapter 1 1
2. Chapter 2 8
3. Chapter 3 16
4. Chapter 4 26
5. Chapter 5 35
6. Chapter 6 43
7. Chapter 7 51
8. Chapter 8 59
9. Chapter 9 70
10. Chapter 10 80
11. Chapter 11 89
12. Chapter 12 99
13. Chapter 13 109
14. Chapter 14 119
15. Chapter 15 129

16. Chapter 16   138

17. Chapter 17   145

18. Chapter 18   154

19. Epilogue   166

CHAPTER 1

There was a girl who went by the name Juniper Stauff. She liked to think of herself as a hero for she solved most of the disputes that were held within the walls of Phantom High. She loved the feeling of being able to help another person out.

Phantom High was situated in Sereneigo and like any other school it did not vary in many ways; its corridors were endlessly bustling with people. Juniper Stauff hated crowds but she pretended not to.

Taking in a deep breath she plastered a smile on her lips and pushed open the doors. The loud noise that filled her ears was horrible but she bit down her disgust and walked on. She walked along the corridor with a smile stuck to her face as she greeted the people she passed.

That was Juniper Stauff. The always out-going, happy, carefree girl. If people were to find out about the numerous things that she hated they would be surprised. She was never known to hate anything. People often thought love was her middle name.

"Hey June," Amanda greeted once Juniper reached her locker.

Juniper was such a crazy name. She had no idea why her parents would ever give her that name. All that was left of her true parents was a bracelet that was currently sitting on her wrist. It had the name JUNIPER engraved onto a rectangular shaped charm.

"Hi Mandy," Juniper smiled back. "What's up?"

"I can't seem to find Dimitri," Amanda said as she shifted from foot to foot. She looked rather nervous, Juniper thought.

"Relax Mandy," smiled Juniper, "he's probably in the library."

"Library. Yes, of course," she laughed but it seemed awfully fake, "I'm so stupid."

"I can't disagree with a fact," Juniper winked as Amanda giggled, rolling her eyes.

"Are you heading to the library?" Amanda asked.

"Yeah," replied Juniper as she put her backpack into the locker. She hated carrying it to class. "Do you want me to pass Dimitri a message?" Again, she added in her head.

"Yes, please. Tell him to meet me in the Janitor's Closet. I've got a little surprise for him."

"Sure thing," she smiled.

"Thanks, June!" Amanda chirped patting Juniper's shoulder. There was something off about her. "You're the best."

"Any time Mandy," Juniper said quietly as she watched Amanda leave. To everyone it would seem as if Amanda and Juniper were close friends. Little they know that Amanda was on Juniper's 'most hated' list. There was something about Amanda that Juniper despised. Maybe it had to do with the fact that she was dating Juniper crush, Dimitri Remirez. Nonetheless, she hated Amanda's guts. And nothing would change that. Juniper was yet to find out the worth of their friendship which she deemed unimportant and insignificant.

"So," drawled Juniper as she attempted to make conversation, the silence slightly irking her. "How's that project coming along?"

Dimitri Remirez looked up from his work. Juniper thought he looked cute. Then again, she had always thought he looked cute. He held a pen between his teeth while another pen sat on his right ear, abandoned and forgotten. He had a thin face and his brown hair was tousled. Juniper held in the urge to run her fingers through his hair. A thick pair of glasses sat on his nose and he looked adorably cute with them. He looked like a nerd but he wasn't. Juniper knew he was failing most of his classes.

Juniper loved it when he wore his glasses but he seldom did so. He usually stuck with his contact lenses because Amanda hated those dorky glasses.

"Not good," Dimitri replied as he pulled the pen out of the grip of his teeth. "I've got like seven books to go through and I'm not even through with the first book. And I've been imprisoned in this library for more than an hour."

"I thought you loved the library," Juniper chuckled at his response.

"I do. Just not when I have projects to do. Then it's boring," he complained.

"Want me to help?" she offered because the novel she was reading was quite boring. She never knew why Dimitri liked these sort of novels. They weren't exciting. Maybe Fantasy wasn't her genre but she wanted to prove something to him - what it was, she wasn't quite sure.

"No," he sighed, running his hand through his hair. "That's alright. How's the book?" He jerked his head towards the novel Juniper was supposedly reading.

She looked confused for a second before realising what he talking about. "Oh yes! This book is amazing," she smiled trying to act as enthusiastic as she could.

"I told you, didn't I?" he smirked buying her fake enthusiasm.

"Totally," she agreed before deciding she didn't want to stay on this topic any longer. "I almost forgot," she said, "Mandy asked me to send you a message-"

Dimitri looked at her with those brown eyes of his. He looked disappointed. "She can't make it?" After a short pause, he added, "again?"

"No," Juniper replied. "She wants you to meet her in the Janitor's closet. She said that she's got a surprise for you."

"She does?" he perked up. Juniper didn't like the way his eyes sparkled. What was it that he saw in Amanda and not her?

"Apparently so," Juniper said disgusted by the images that flickered into her mind.

"Why didn't you tell me this when you came into the library?" he asked.

Juniper shrugged, the lie slipping through her mouth effortlessly. "You looked busy."

He rolled his eyes. "Okay, I guess I'll see you later?"

"Definitely," Juniper smiled despite the aching feeling in her chest. Dimitri packed his things quickly and threw Juniper one last smile before he got up from the table they were sharing and left. If only he knew what that smile did to her.

As Dimitri Remirez made his way to the Janitor's closet he couldn't stop smiling. For reasons unknown, Amanda was acting pretty distant the past few days. Every time Dimitri and her were to hang out, she'd bail on him the last minute.

This is how Dimitri Remirez and Amanda Obereen started out:

Dimitri always admired Amanda. He didn't know what it was about her that he felt attracted to. Was it her beauty? Or was it her personality? Maybe it was her intelligence. Dimitri simply didn't know. All he did know was the he liked Amanda so much so that he finally grew a pair and asked her out.

Amanda said no at first and though he was disappointed at her response he was not all that sad. He had, after all, expected it. Why would a girl like her date a boy like him?

But later that very day that he asked her out she came up to him and told him that she made a mistake; that she wanted to go out with him.

Dimitri didn't believe her at the beginning but after their first date he didn't care how quickly her mind had changed. He would always remember their first date. The minute they sat down in McDonald's there was something that instantly clicked between them. Everything that spilled out of Amanda's mouth made Dimitri happy. And the way Amanda was smiling - he'd never seen her smile so lovely before. He loved the way that she'd always pour out her feelings to him when she was angry or sad or simply joyful. He didn't quite understand the things she talked about sometimes but he loved the way that she didn't give in to the problems in her life. In simple words, he adored her confidence.

They made each other happy and that was all Dimitri cared about. Amanda was the only person he let see his demons. And suddenly with Amanda in his life, his home life seemed much more bearable. Painful but a little more bearable.

So after numerous dates, shared feelings and a few kisses he asked her to be his girlfriend. There was that pleasing glint in her eyes that made him extremely happy. Dimitri could tell that over the time that they spent together Amanda changed for the better.

His affection for her grew into something more and it wasn't until a few days ago that he decided he should confess. He remembered the day so clearly.

"Amanda, I need to tell you something," he had said.

They were sitting on a blanket looking up at the stars. Amanda turned her head so she was facing him and giving him her undivided attention. "What is it?" she smiled.

"Mandy," Dimitri started. He then took her hands into his and stared into those beautiful eyes of hers saying the three words that was sure to change the world they shared. "I love you."

Her eyes had begun to tear up and her lovely lips cracked into a smile. "Oh my god," she gushed before throwing her arms around his neck, excitedly. Dimitri hugged her back and smiled, satisfied at the reaction he had got.

She pulled back and looked up at him. "I love-" she started but stopped mid-way. The expression on her face changed as if she were remembering something horrible.

Dimitri's smile slipped off his face as they stared at each other. It was as if she wanted to say those precious words back to him but something was holding her back.

"Why won't you say it?' he asked.

Silence was his reply. "Come on," she finally said breaking the ear-piercing silence. "I think it's best if we head home."

And from that day Amanda started to act strange. She ditched dates that Dimitri and her were to go on and she'd always send Juniper to tell him that she couldn't make it. Dimitri knew that he had made a grave mistake by telling the love of his life how he truly felt.

But the fact that Amanda wanted to meet Dimitri in the Janitor's closet excited him. Maybe she was going to give him another chance and they were finally going to move on from that disaster.

Dimitri's hope went to waste.

He rounded the bend that lead to the Janitor's closet and stopped short. The noise emerging from the room seemed rather inappropriate and disturbing and he thought Juniper might have given him the wrong message.

But she didn't. It wasn't until he opened the door did he discover that Juniper delivered the message clearly.

He opened the door and the blood ran from his face and he froze, confusion written across his face. His eyes bulged as he watched the scene unravel before his eyes. He stood there emotionless as he tried to decipher was was happening.

A girl and a boy were going at each other in a way that was probably thought illegal. The girl had her long, dark legs around the boy's waist and the boy had her up against the wall, grinding into her as he massaged the girl's thigh.

It took Dimitri less time to recognise the boy. It was Charlie Cox, infamous football player and often the talk of the school.

Dimitri finally recognised the girl and he was left more confused than ever. His heart began to race faster and his face morphed into one of disbelief, and anger lingered somewhere within that mask of confusion.

Then he finally spoke up, voicing his confusion. "Amanda?"

CHAPTER 2

Dimitri Remirez leaned against the hood of his car as he looked up at the sky. His car was neither fashionable nor comfortable. It was run down, with useless pieces of metal assembled together. The engine was blasted and it took - what seemed to Dimitri - hours to make the car work. The car probably needed to be refuelled at least twice a day. In simple words it was a very crappy car.

Why was the universe always against him? His life at home was torturous and he thought Amanda could make it better. And she did. But now even that was taken away from him. He couldn't understand what he did to deserve this?

Amanda and him were getting along perfectly well. He should have know better and kept his mouth shut. If he had not told her that he loved her maybe that that wouldn't have driven her away. That was the fatal flaw in their relationship; Dimitri's love. At least that was what he thought.

He continued to stare at the sky, his sight blurring every few seconds as he mulled over the past and spotted out the mistakes, flaws, things he should have not done to make her turn away from him.

And then it suddenly hit him like he was splashed with ice cold water. Amanda and Dimitri would always enjoy themselves and just like that, in an instant, Dimitri was viewing everything in a new angle. Everything she did was fake.

They set him up. Dimitri Remirez was a joke. And even if Amanda Obereen liked Dimitri, it simply didn't matter. People would do anything for popularity and for Amanda that was humiliating Dimitri. True feelings were simply set aside. True feelings were seen as the evil while popularity as the good.

"Argh!" Dimitri exclaimed at last as he let out all his anger into a kick against his car. Tears begun to gather in his eyes and he fisted his hand as he tried to keep his anger in check. "Dad's right. I'm a fool," he said so softly that he could not even hear his own delicate whisper.

He blinked rapidly trying to rid any tears before they spilt over. How could he be such a fool?

"Hi!" Juniper chirped as she jumped in front of Dimitri.

He jumped a little startled by her actions as he stared at the blonde haired girl that stood before him. She always kept dying her hair. One week it was blonde and then the following week it would be a dark red, almost a brown colour. Dimitri could never decide what colour she looked better with. "What's up, Dimmy?" Juniper nudged as leaned against the hood of his car beside Dimitri, smiling as always.

What Dimitri would never be able to understand was how Juniper Stauff could be cheerful and happy and always full of joy. Did she ever feel sad or even lonely or not content with life?

"Don't call me Dimmy," he said, his voice low and it almost sounded hostile.

"You love being called Dimmy," she argued.

"No," he said giving her a pointed look. "I hate it."

"But it's unique. And special," she winked.

"How so?" he questioned.

"Because I'm the only one who calls you Dimmy."

Dimitri chuckled at his best friend's response. "Shut up."

"Is that a smile I see?" Juniper teased. "Oh my god. Someone needs to take a picture of this. The Great Juniper Stauff has made The Grumpy Dimitri Remirez laugh. I am amazing. Don't you agree?"

Dimitri could not stop himself from laughing. He bumped his shoulder with hers, a smile slipping and framing his adorable features. "Shut up."

"You and I both know that that's impossible," she smirked confidently.

Dimitri towered above her, his gaze on her somewhat curious. "Nothing is impossible," he said.

They stared at each other until Dimitri's facial expression grew into one of that of sadness. He returned back to his previous position, staring up at the sky. "Did you know that this was all some stupid plan to hurt me?" he asked Juniper as he continued to stare at the sky, afraid that if he looked back at her his eyes would betray him and he would break down.

She shifted uncomfortably beside him. "What are you talking about?"

"Cut the crap, June," he said, his voice laced with betrayal and annoyance.

Juniper took a deep breath before she faced him again. "Yes, I knew-"

"You did? Why didn't you-"

"Hey!" she said breaking his sentence off so she could defend herself. "I suspected it. Mandy didn't come and tell me herself. I would've told you immediately if she did. Plus, even if I did try and tell you my suspicions you'd never listen. You'd probably think I was some self-centred bitch or somewhat jealous!"

"Self-centred bitch?" Dimitri echoed. "Do you hear yourself? I mean, you're the Juniper Stauff. You couldn't even be a bitch if you tried."

"I don't know why but I find that offensive," Juniper said.

He chuckled. "And jealous? Why would I think that you'd be jealous? June, you have everything you've ever wanted."

She looked into those brown of his. "You have no idea how wrong you are, do you?"

His brows furrowed. This was not the Juniper Stauff he knew. She looked away and he pushed back on his car with his foot so he could bounce back with support as he stood in front of her. "June?"

"What?" she said looking up at him. She was not smiling and that took Dimitri completely by surprise.

"What's wrong?" he asked.

"Nothing. Why would you assume that anything is wrong?"

"Because you-"

"Dimmy?"

"Yeah?"

Juniper looked at Dimitri and there it was again. That longing look. That look was there since the beginning of their friendship and Dimitri could never understand what it meant.

"Just forget it," she whispered, her voice cracking in the process.

He looked at her, words momentarily failing him. He wanted to know what had upset her but even though he had never seen this side of Juniper, he knew pressing this issue would only make her more upset. So he said, "forget what?"

She smiled and brought her arms around his thin waist, hugging him out of gratitude. She had then put her hand on top of his head and messed his hair. "You're so cute, Dimmy," she grinned.

"Why, thank you, Miss Stauff," Dimitri grinned back as he did a small curtsey.

They laughed, Juniper's comments amusing them. Juniper stopped in mid-laugh and there was a glint in her eyes which Dimitri immediately disapproved of once he saw it.

"Oh no," he said as he shook his head before she could say anything.

"What?"

"I know that look. It's that same look you have when you figure out a way to help cheat on a test or make me look stupid. So whatever it is; no," Dimitri deadpanned.

"But you haven't even heard what I have to say," complained Juniper.

Dimitri scrunched his face, his mind at battle. "Okay," he finally said. "What's up?"

"I'm sorry that Mandy and you didn't work out as you wanted-"

"June, we're over this-"

"No we're not, Dimitri!" Juniper exclaimed. Juniper was full of surprises and Dimitri was not aware of this side of his best friend until that day. "She broke your heart for no good reason-"

"I'm pretty sure she had a reason," Dimitri defended.

"Seriously?" Juniper looked at Dimitri with disbelief. "After that harsh break up you're still defending her?" Why she looked slightly disappointed, Dimitri could not have told at that time.

"June, you don't understand-"

"You're such a-"

"I loved her!" shouted Dimitri. Juniper cowered at the tone of his voice. Dimitri lowered his voice and said, "I loved her, okay? And I still love her, June."

Juniper looked up at Dimitri and hurt swarmed in her eyes. Dimitri had not known why she would be hurt. Maybe it was because he raised his voice against hers but Dimitri knew better. He knew that a simple change of tone would not hurt Juniper. It would take much more than that to hurt her.

"And when I found her in the Janitor's closet with Charlie Cox-" he broke off, tears gathering in his eyes. He looked away. He hadn't wanted Juniper to witness him this weak. "I don't know why it is that I love her. Even after that cruel joke she played on me I still love her. Love doesn't go away fast as it comes. I love Amanda Obereen. That's why I defend her even though she proved to be an absolute bitch today."

Juniper looked up at Dimitri. "I'm sorry," she said so low that he could barely hear her. "But I still think my idea is genius."

"Okay," sighed Dimitri. "What's this 'genius' idea of yours?"

"It's simple." Then she paused before she said the two words that Dimitri never thought he'd live to see the day that she'd utter those words so effortlessly. "Take revenge."

His eyes bulged and he stared at her for what seemed like a life time. "Excuse me?" he said straining his ears thinking that he had heard wrong.

She simply chuckled. "You heard right, Dimmy," she smiled.

"Wow." Dimitri could not quite believe his ears. What Juniper suggested was not only insane but also not very Juniper-like thing to do nor say. Was she even capable of revenge? "I never thought I'd live to to see the day Juniper Stauff would seek revenge," Dimitri said, still dazed.

"What's so surprising about me wanting revenge because some hot headed girl broke my best friend's heart?" she asked before she looked up at him for an answer.

He raised his brows at her. "You are seriously asking me that? You are Juniper Stauff. The only 'bad' you can commit in your life is help me cheat on a test. Otherwise you are all 'good'. Last time I checked revenge was categorised under 'bad'."

Juniper smiled. "People often confuse the term bad or evil with justice. Dimmy, revenge is justice." Dimitri simply stared at the girl in front of him, at a loss for words.

"Well," she sighed. "This was a good talk. I should be heading home before-"

Dimitri reached out and gripped her hand, not letting her escape. He simply couldn't process her outrageous suggestion. "I'm not going to take revenge on my girlfriend," he said sternly.

"Ex-girlfriend," she corrected him. "And why the hell not?"

"It's not right, June," he said.

Juniper removed her hand from Dimitri's grip and smiled. "You're just very emotional right now. You love her, I get that. But what she did to you..? Dimitri that is cruelty and she deserves justice. I don't have a solid plan right now but give me a couple of hours or a day and I will come up with something." When she saw the uncertainty in his eyes, she said, " think about it, okay? I'll see you tomorrow, Dimmy."

She gave him one last smile before she leaned away from the hood of Dimitri's car and walked away. Dimitri watched her figure grow smaller and smaller. Her words echoed loud in his head and he couldn't decide if she was right or if she was wrong.

Chapter 3

Dimitri Remirez and his father sat down for dinner. Their dinners were often filled with silence and tension. Dimitri feared his father. Since the age of ten - since the time of his mother's departure - he was being abused but his father. Mr Remirez would never dare hurt his son's face in fear that other people would see Dimitri's scars.

"Finals are approaching fast," Mr Remirez said. Dimitri looked up from his food and gulped hard. He knew what was coming next. "How are your current grades?"

Dimitri looked at his father. "Oh, you know. They're fairly good-"

"What's your current grade in ICT?" Mr Remirez asked as he took a swig of his beer bottle, his drunken gaze on his son.

"A," Dimitri replied, looking at his father through his lashes as he feared that looking directly into his father's eyes would smoulder him.

"And your English grade?"

Dimitri's heart began to race a marathon. The scars on his body suddenly seemed to burn. He was remembering the previous night.

"Well, English is categorised," he explained as he looked down at his plate. He had taken no more than three bites from his food. He always hated spaghetti and maybe the reason for his hate towards spaghetti was because his mother loved it. "There's English Literature and English Language and though the grade is put together, I think it's quite unfair that-"

"I don't give a damn of what you think is fair!" Mr Remirez shouted as he banged his beer bottle against the weak dining table in the kitchen. He lifted the beer bottle towards his lips and took another swig. "What's your English grade, Dimitri?"

Each word dropped out Dimitri's father's mouth like venom; poison; ready to kill. Dimitri shifted his food around with his fork as both fear and anxiousness began to settle in the pit of his stomach. "D," he said so low that his father was unable to hear him.

"Speak louder," Mr Remirez bellowed.

Dimitri took a deep breath before answering. "My current garde in English is a D...dad." He hoped that adding 'dad' at the end would make his punishment less harsh. Mr Remirez stopped seeing Dimitri as his son and more as his slave eight years ago - the instant his wife took off.

"That's ironic," Mr Remirez laughed. "With the countless hours that you spend in the library anyone would think that you'd excel in English. Oh, how wrong they are about you. You're a failure, Dimitri; a burden that I must forever carry."

Dimitri felt like crying. He bit down on his bottom lip as he forced the tears back so he could show to his father that he was not a wimp, that he was brave. "I'm sorry, dad."

Mr Remirez laughed. "Dad," he mused ,"why do you call me that?"

Dimitri was momentarily shocked and he felt as if a bucket of ice, cold water was poured on top of him. This was the first time that he was approached by this subject directly by his father. "You're my father-"

"Me? How are you so sure?"

Dimitri straightened in his chair and looked up at his father, confused by his antics. "What do you mean?"

"You're mother is a bitch, Dimitri," Mr Remirez said as he took another swig from his bottle. Dimitri fisted his hands and his blood began to boil. The more Mr Remirez spoke, the angrier Dimitri got. "How do I know that she's not been sleeping around? That you're actually my child?"

"There's something called a DNA test," Dimitri lashed out without thinking what he was saying. "Did you forget that this was the 21st century, dad?"

Mr Remirez got up from his chair and tossed it back, the vein on his neck popping out as the anger from the insult his son threw in his face coursed through his body. "Say that again," Mr Remirez ordered.

He approached his son taking slow and menacing steps forward. Fear coursed through Dimitri and he quickly scrambled off his chair looking for an escape even though he should have known better, that there was simply no escape from his father.

"Say that again!" Mr Remirez shouted once more.

"There's s-something c-called a D-DNA test," Dimitri stuttered as he backed up into a corner of the kitchen and he wished the walls to close around him and protect his frail body from his father. He watched his father's every move with fearful eyes.

"You said something after that, didn't you?"

Dimitri shook his head rapidly. "I didn't say anyt-"

He doubled over as his father slashed his beer bottle down the right side of Dimitri's face, the liquid staining his face. He could even taste the bitter sample of beer that had entered his mouth and burned his throat. His hand flew up to his face, his trembling fingers tracing the blood that flowed from the corner of his eye, down through the right side of his cheek, stopping just above his lips.

He looked up at his father with new emotion swimming in his eyes. He had never felt more afraid in his life than he did right then. New tears sprung into his eyes shamelessly. He didn't care if his father saw them. The scar that was yet to grace his face burned with such intensity that it changed every view he had of his father.

"Lair!" Mr Remirez roared which made Dimitri cower back against the wall. He stepped closer and lifted Dimitri's face with his long, icy index finger. "I would never hurt that precious face of yours but when you talk back to me like that, something you have never even attempted to do, then isn't it worth the risk, son?"

Dimitri was scared but at the same time a sudden rush of anger coursed beneath his skin. "I thought you said I wasn't your son," he said, his voice cracking as he spoke.

He had not known what happened next but in an instant he found himself on the floor of the kitchen, his body aching with pain. Mr Remirez towered above him. "Don't you dare talk back to me like that!" he yelled.

"Don't you dare call mum a bitch!" Dimitri fought back as he draped his arm around his stomach.

Mr Remirez raised his foot and kicked Dimitri's aching side making his son's body shrivel with pain. The tears in Dimitri's eyes split over as the searing pain grew worse. He felt the anger wash out of him all at once as his mind was consumed in terror. He curled into a ball, holding his hands up at his father as he begged. "Stop...please," he cried out desperately.

Mr Remirez smirked at the response he got. "Don't be weak. I thought I taught you better. Now go and get cleaned up. I'm heading out to the bar. I won't be home till late." And then he left his son withering on the kitchen floor.

Dimitri pulled up his strength and forced himself to get up once he heard the loud bang which indicated that his father had vacated the house. He staggered up the stairs, using the railing as support. Once he closed the door to his room behind him, he leaned against it, his legs failing to carry him to the bathroom. He touched the side of his face and winced as the searing pain shot at him.

He then looked across the room and froze.

There stood a dark-haired girl going through his bookshelf smiling upon every title that she read. There stood the girl that was recently full of surprises - a girl Dimitri least thought would be full of surprises.

He blinked rapidly. Finally, he broke the silence. "June?"

Juniper Stauff had come up with a brilliant plan and she couldn't wait to share it with Dimitri. But Dimitri wasn't answering her texts or calls. This was very expected of Dimitri. Why did he even have a phone when half the time it was off? That's why Juniper was set as Amanda's messenger to Dimitri.

Juniper was growing impatient with her underdeveloped, plot-hole-filled plan. So she decided to go to his place. When she arrived there she heard strangled voices, shouts and words that she could not decipher. Nonetheless, the noises she heard were pretty awful but something told her that she should mind her own business.

She looked for a ladder in the garden shack, put it up against the wall and climbed up to Dimitri's room. Fortunately, he had left the window open.

His bookshelf immediately captivated her. There was the Harry Potter series, The Lord of the Rings series, the Percy Jackson series and many other stand alone novels. She skimmed through the bookshelf with her index finger fascinated by how many books Dimitri had. Some she had read before and some she never knew existed. You can't blame her. She had never taken a liking to novels.

"Juniper?" a strangled voice spoke up.

She jumped, startled and held a hand to her chest. "You almost scared the living shit out of me, Dimmy," she said, her eyes not wavering from the bookshelf.

"I scared you? Says Juniper The Robber," Dimitri scoffed.

"Oh, I am definitely here to rob. This bookshelf looks amazeballs," she said in an awestruck voice as she gestured at the magnificent bookshelf.

"Amazeballs isn't a word, June," he said, his voice sounding strangled again.

Juniper turned to face her best friend and a gasp caught stuck in her throat. Her jaw dropped as she kept on staring at the broken boy. "Holy shitstickers," she said, dazed.

"Shitstickers? That's not a word either. I think I know what I'm buying for your birthd-" Dimitri never got to finish his sentence. He fell to the floor and his face scrunched in pain.

Juniper rushed forward to aid her best friend. "Oh my god, oh my god, oh my god," she panicked. "Dimmy, don't die!"

Dimitri chuckled then coughed. "Help me get to the bathroom?" he asked, his voice took an urgent tone. "The first aid kit is in the top cabinet."

Juniper let out a huff of breath. "Okay, June," she told herself. "You can fix this." She then helped Dimitri get to the bathtub and clean out his wounds. She was fascinated - in a horrid way - by the scars that covered his torso.

And she couldn't stop her mind from wondering: how did Dimitri get these marks? And why would the person she had begun to suspect do this to him?

After Juniper helped Dimitri sit down on his bed, she took a seat beside him. She stared at his face and Dimitri felt slightly agitated by the way that she looked at him. "What?" he asked. "Why are you looking at me like that?"

Instead of answering Dimitri, Juniper had lifted her hand to the right side of his face. He winced but after a couple of seconds he let her touch the scorching burn; the ugly scar. It hurt when she touched it but he welcomed the care anyway. "Who did this to you?" Juniper asked.

Dimitri looked down at the innocent girl. She sounded sad. "It doesn't matter," he said, his voice holding a bored and monotonous tone to it.

Juniper's expression turned into one of that of disbelief and anger. "Doesn't matter?" she echoed almost screaming. If his father were still in the house he would be fearful that she was speaking with such a loud voice. "Okay. You're freaking girlfriend doesn't matter, what she did to you doesn't matter. This monster who tortured you like this doesn't matter. So tell me, Dimmy, what does matter to you?"

Dimitri kept silent. He could not answer her without giving everything away and his burden was not one that he was willing to share with his best friend. He looked away, her face holding so much accusation he could not contain his own guilt.

She sighed. "How long has this been happening?" When silence was her reply, she scoffed. "Let me guess. It doesn't matter."

She was angry. That much Dimitri could tell. He was desperate to change the subject. "Just today your hair was blonde. You already dyed it red?" he asked turning back to face her.

Juniper was disappointed and her looks mirrored her emotions perfectly. "I hate when you do this," she said.

"Do what?" Dimitri asked.

"You always change the subject when you feel uncomfortable - when you're too afraid to talk about what's bugging you."

"I'm not afraid."

"Yeah?" she questioned. "Then why won't you talk to me?" He didn't reply and when she realised that Dimitri wasn't going to answer her most curious questions, she turned away from him. "My plan. I dyed my hair because of my plan," she said. "I thought it was best that you take revenge at night and blonde was too bright of a colour."

Juniper looked at Dimitri who had his eyes wide open and his mouth agape.

"What? Red's a darker colour," she defended.

"My revenge?" Dimitri asked, his voice holding uncertainty.

"It is your revenge," Juniper said in somewhat of a confirmation tone.

"June, I'm not taking part in this crazy plan of yours-"

"Why won't you let me help?!" she exclaimed. She was up in an instant and she stood in front of Dimitri so he could see the clear fury that shone brilliantly in her eyes. "I want to help. Why won't you let me in? You let Mandy in who, by the way, only knows you for - what? - nine months? And I've known you my entire life, since bloody Kindergarten. After you're tenth birthday something about you felt a bit off to me. You looked broken and you grew more secretive. The point of us vowing to be best friends in Kindergarten was that we would tell each other every fucking thing and help each other." Her words held a hint of betrayal but Dimitri at that time had not known that nor would he ever know.

"You only share what has to be shared and you bear whatever else pain by yourself. And I've always wanted to help. So why won't you let me in? Why won't you let me help? Why, Dimmy?"

Dimitri looked up at Juniper in amazement. She noticed the change in his turning point of life. How long was it going to take for her to figure out everything else; to see his demons and the burden he had to carry? Sudden thoughts as these were what made up Dimitri's mind.

"Alright," he said, cracking a smile as he spoke. "I'm in on the plan."

Juniper looked uncertain and a bit disappointed at the reaction she got but then she rolled her eyes and squealed. She bent down and hugged the living daylights out of Dimitri. He grunted when the pain shot up his abdomen and she immediately let go which resulted him falling back on the bed with a soft thud.

"Oops," she grinned cheesily.

Dimitri chuckled. He loved the quirky side of Juniper. Despite them being best friends he had not known of the existence of the much darker side of Juniper. It wasn't going to take much time from this incident for him to witness it.

"I gotta go," she said, looking at the clock on Dimitri's wall. "It's almost ten and I still have homework to finish. Meet me by my locker before first period and I'll tell you everything! I was going to tell you now but I think it's best if you rest. Maybe you shouldn't come to school tomorrow-"

"No, I'll be coming to school." Struggling slightly, he stood up and followed Juniper to the window. "Oh," he said as he looked out the window to see a ladder leaning against the wall. "That's how you got up."

"Unfortunately, I can't fly so I had to use a ladder," she mused, scrunching her brows in fake frustration.

"Goodnight," he laughed, leaning down and pecking her cheek.

"You sure you want to come to school tomorrow? Missing a day of school won't cost anything-"

It'll cost torture from my father, Dimitri thought bitterly. "I'll see you tomorrow," he promised.

With a hesitant nod she leaned forward and returned his kiss by pecking her lips on his forehead. "Get better. And sleep, or I'll kill you. Bye!" Juniper chirped, smiling at her best friend before climbing down the ladder.

The smile on Dimitri's face slowly slipped off his face as he watched her retreating figure. "Oh Juniper," he whispered to himself. "What are you getting me involved in?"

CHAPTER 4

The following day Dimitri Remirez scoured the school corridors for Juniper. The pain in his abdomen had slowly subsided but some of it still remained and he was wincing from time to time. Remembering that Juniper had told him to meet him by her locker, he turned around and headed in that direction trying as hard as he could to avoid the stares that were being given to him.

The scar on Dimitri's face still looked fresh and harsh and every person that he passed along the corridor stopped whatever they were doing to look at him. Some had pitying looks in their eyes. Maybe they thought he was mourning over losing the love of his life to a total jerk by hurting himself. If they were actual friends of Dimitri they would know better than to assume ludicrous things like that.

Dimitri has tossed and turned around in bed until he finally came up to a conclusion and made up his mind about this plan of Juniper's. He was not taking part in it.

He had no idea what Juniper had in store and this girl had recently started booming with surprises. What if she planned something in this revenge that Dimitri did not approve of? In that moment he may have not liked Amanda Obereen for breaking his heart but he would never do anything to hurt her, whether it be physically or emotionally.

He walked along the corridor and when he spotted her by her locker, his heart deflated. She was not alone.

Dimitri wanted to avoid awkward situations and so he was half turned around ready to leave. Unfortunately, Juniper had already seen him and started to wave him over. He let out a sigh. He had no choice, really. Juniper was bubbling with excitement and Dimitri knew why. He hated himself for being the person who was about to break that little bubble of hers.

"Hey," he greeted as he looked at Juniper and gave her companion a nod of acknowledgement. When he looked at her face he was unable to muster any words. Amanda Obereen looked devastated but beautiful at the same time.

"Hey-lo," Juniper chirped with a smile on her face before she frowned as she noticed the sudden tensed atmosphere. "Oh," was all she could say.

Amanda looked at Dimitri and almost immediately her face fell as her eyes glazed over Dimitri's new scar. She looked sad and looked like she was about to cry. She knew. Dimitri knew that she knew. Words didn't have to be spoken for Amanda to understand how he had gotten that scar and who gave it to him. This would have been the time when Amanda would pull him into a cuddly, bear hug and kiss the living daylights out of him. She would try anything to subside his pain and in that moment Dimitri knew she would not do anything to comfort him. She would not even touch him. And, truthfully, he hated her for that.

How could she choose popularity over me, he thought, his entire being reeled with spite. When did she become so materialistic?

"I got to go," Amanda said as she gave Juniper a smile but her eyes held clear sorrow. With not a second glance at her ex-boyfriend, she dashed down the corridor, rushing into the girls wash-room.

She chose popularity. Dimitri could not get it out of his head. He loved her and he still did and he knew that she felt the same strong emotion that he had for her. She almost said it, those three beautiful words - I love you - but it seemed like ages ago to Dimitri. She cared more for her popularity. She chose it over Dimitri and he could not shake off the horrific thought no matter how bad he wanted to.

"So," Juniper drawled making Dimitri snap his attention back to her. "I need to tell you about the plan and I-"

"No."

"What?" Juniper asked taken aback.

"June, I'm dropping out of this crazy plan of yours-"

"But you don't know what it is," Juniper whined.

"And I don't need to. I am not going to hurt Amanda."

"I still don't understand why you love her, Dimmy," Juniper said in a small voice and he was, again, surprised by her strange behaviour. She leaned on her locker and looked up at him. Then something flashed across her eyes and Dimitri immediately knew she was cooking something new up. Juniper's plans for revenge that night were ruined but not entirely.

"There's no changing your mind, is there?" she asked, almost challengingly.

Dimitri Remirez gave her a firm nod. "Absolutely not."

Juniper smiled and left Dimitri standing by her locker with the words, "we'll see about that," hanging fresh in the air.

There was a light bang on the table and Dimitri looked up to see a perky Juniper. When was she not perky? She sat down, giddy, waiting for Dimitri to ask her why she was in such a happy mood. When he didn't, she said, "guess what?"

Something was up with Juniper, Dimitri could tell. "I'd rather not," he said, burying his face further into the novel he was reading. He still had his assignment to finish but the novel he was reading was more interesting than the boring assignment.

She rolled her eyes. "Tonight. 7 PM. Party as Brooke's. Pick me up?"

"What?" he asked as he was slightly confused by the sudden and too rushed information. He lifted his head from the novel and set the book aside. His urge to read on into the mystery novel was gone and instead Juniper's words rang loud in his ears.

"Brooke's parents are away for the week so he's having a party tonight. You seem all tensed up and I thought maybe you would like to let off some air and have other things on your mind, get a little drunk and dance maybe."

"I can't dance," Dimitri said and Juniper knew that was his way of declining her request.

Juniper Stauff ignored it. "I know. Remember the seventh grade rehearsal? God, you were horrible."

"Hence why I didn't make it to the final cut," Dimitri smiled when he heard Juniper giggle at his response.

They were reminiscing over their seventh grade play. Auditions were held and there was a dance scene that particularly interested Dimitri and he wanted to get himself into that scene. Juniper was his partner and turns out he was not the dance expert he claimed to be.

Juniper returned her focus back to the present. "So? What do you think of my proposal?" she grinned as she propped her arms forward and lay her chin on the back of her hands.

"No," Dimitri shook his head. "I'm exhausted." The truth was that he was afraid of his father. What if his father was home for dinner and he didn't find his son there? Dimitri would not live to even take a glimpse of daylight again if so.

Juniper pouted. "Come on," she urged. "Ugh, you're no fun."

"Excuse you, I'm plenty of fun," he defended playfully.

"Is that so?" Juniper sad pretending to be innocent.

Dimitri looked at her. He sighed. If only she could stop looking at him like that. She had that dazzle in her eyes and did that pout thing with her mouth that made Dimitri feel guilty for declining. "Fine," he surrendered.

"You're coming?" The excitement in her voice rang clear.

"Um," he paused. "I'll think about it."

Juniper Stauff stood in front of the mirror admiring herself in the short black dress. She looked dashing and absolutely beautiful. And she knew that. But was that enough to impress Dimitri? No. He was still in love with Amanda and that crude joke she played on Dimitri did not seem to faze his love for her at all.

How could he be so blind? she thought. But Juniper could not bring herself to entirely blame him. Before she became the couple's messenger, she actually thought they were in love. In fact, she knew that they are still in love. They looked so happy with each other.

Juniper did not have any enemies. Everybody loved her. She was the picture perfect girl and definition of cliché. Everybody thought that she had everything that she ever wanted. But she didn't.

She sat down on her bed waiting patiently for Dimitri. She absent-mindedly played with the charm that laid on her bracelet. Her parents. She had no idea who they were. She had only met them once and when she met them, she wished she would never see them again. All that she was told was that she was put into an adopting care centre at the age of two. There she spent a couple of years before a barren couple decided to adopt her.

Juniper grew closer to her adoptive family and it was not too long until she started calling her adoptive parents mum and dad. She remembered, once upon a time, she was embarrassed of them. All the children in her class had proper parents; parents with the same race as their child. Juniper did not have that. She was very fair in complexion compared to her adoptive parents' dark chocolate skin tone.

But Juniper grew to love the fact that her adoptive parents were of a completely different race than she was. It kind of distinguished her from other children and that made her feel unique and special. She could never thank them enough for all they have done and given her. She loved them endlessly.

And then there was Dimitri Remirez. Their friendship blossomed ever since they fought over a swing in Kindergarten. From that day on Dimitri made it life mission to get to know Juniper. Up until the age of ten that is. He disappeared from school and the face of the planet for a few weeks before appearing back and acting like nothing had happened. He had looked horrible. He still looked cute and adorable in Juniper's eyes but there had been a drastic change within him, Juniper could tell. He cared less, he kept to himself more and spent most of his time in the library reading. Juniper knew reading novels was his way of an escape. But an escape from what?

Juniper clenched her hand remembering the previous night. Dimitri looked so battered and bruised she could almost swear she heard her heart shatter. She suspected his father had done this to Dimitri but why would he...how could he? That was his own son.

Juniper's train of thoughts was immediately cut off when she heard the bell ring. Excitement began to bubble within her. She was going to show Dimitri that she was right, that he deserved his revenge. Juniper was not quite sure why she was so hellbent on helping Dimitri get his revenge, she had hope that things would finally start to go her way, but she hated to see him broken like this - more broken than usual anyway. She hoped that in the process she could win his heart.

Strapping on her four inch heels, because five inches were too much for her to bear, she grabbed her silver purse before rushing downstairs to the door.

When she threw open the door she was delighted with the view that greeted her eyes. There stood Dimitri clad in black, slim jeans that hung low at his hips. He wore a buttoned down grey shirt with the first two buttons unhooked. He had on his favourite converse sneakers.

"You don't look so bad, Dimmy," Juniper smirked giving him a wink. Oh, how badly she wanted to grab him by the collar and kiss him.

"Yeah? Well, you definitely out-dressed me," he said as his eyes travelled down Juniper's body. Juniper was not going to lie to herself. She kind of liked the fact that Dimitri was ogling her. "I thought we were going to some party. You didn't tell me that we were we going to a fashion show and you were a model in the show."

Juniper was flattered and her cheeks grew hot. She knew he didn't mean it in the way she wished it meant but she accepted the compliment anyway.

She rolled her eyes. "Haven't you been to a party before, Dimmy?"

"I have, of course. It's hard not to go to parties when you have Amanda Obereen as your girlfriend," he replied and Juniper detected a little hate in his voice. Good, she thought.

"Ex-girlfriend now," Juniper said as she stepped outside of the house and closed the door behind her. Her parents had gone out for a dinner - it was date night - and left their daughter with the spare key since they weren't going to be back till Saturday, the following morning. She locked the door before tucking the key in her purse. "C'mon," she said heading towards Dimitri's car.

"Wait," Dimitri said as he reached out and held Juniper's wrist firmly with her hand. "Is Mandy going to be there?" he asked.

She did not feel like lying to him but she wanted him to come. She needed to show him that Amanda was not worth his love. So she said, "I don't know. It's Brooke's party. Big crowd, y'know?"

"June, I can't face her," he said.

You're going to have to, she thought. "Who said she'll be there?" Juniper asked.

"There's a big possibility that she does show up..." Dimitri trailed off as his face morphed into one of that of guilt. "Stop doing that!"

Juniper did not stop pouting at him. "Come on," she complained. "I dressed up for yo-" she caught herself quickly in time to correct herself, "this party." Oh god, she almost told him that she had dolled up for him. How embarrassing.

"Fine," he said letting out a sigh. "But if anything happens then it's all your fault."

"Yes sir," Juniper saluted, "I will make sure there are no casualties."

Dimitri rolled his eyes as he ushered her into his car. He had to admit to himself that other than Amanda, Juniper was the only one who could clear his mystic mood.

As they drove to Brenton Brooke's house Juniper smiled. All's going according to plan so far, she thought smugly.

CHAPTER 5

Where on earth did Juniper disappear to?

They had both entered the house together and immediately the stale smell of sweat, heat and alcohol whirled in the air they inhaled. Dimitri had turned his head to scan the crowd to see if he spotted a certain dark haired girl. When he did not see Amanda anywhere within his sight his heart lifted and he breathed out a sigh of relief.

He turned his attention back to Juniper about to ask her to dance with him and save him from embarrassing himself if he danced by himself. He was definitely not a good dancer and Juniper was the one of the best.

But she was no where in sight either. He scanned the crowd once more, this time searching for a different girl. She brought him here. She can't just abandon him.

A few moments later he gave up and headed towards the food table. He picked up a solo cup and filled it with punch. He drank down all the punch in one go, letting the liquid burn his throat. Instantly, he knew it was not punch. It certainly did not taste like punch. It tasted bittersweet and better than punch. And Dimitri poured himself more cups until he could take no more.

His eyes shifted to the dance floor and excitement flooded him. Moving closer to the mob of bodies, he thrust his body in odd angles trying to dance. Let's just face; he can't dance to even save his lift.

He felt a hand a hand lay itself on his chest and he looked up and found a drunken girl, her eyes glowing as she stared at his tall figure. "Don't you look dashing tonight," she slurred.

Disgusted by the girl's behaviour he pushed her away and finally reached the couches. He had thought of dancing but there was no need to embarrass himself further. Hopefully no one saw his attempt to dance a few seconds earlier.

He may have felt a little heavy-headed and a little drunk but he still had his sanity very much intact. Why did he come here? He had absolutely nothing to do. He was not about to drink away his sorrows. No, he was not going to end up like his uncle, Miles Miller. His uncle had been chucked into the loony bin because Miles had somehow escaped sanity. The guilt inside had finally cracked Miles and turned him into a mad man. Dimitri did not want to end up like his uncle. His uncle was a very bad example. Just like his sister; Dimitri's mother.

Where the hell is Juniper? he thought as his eyes scanned the crowd once more. And then he froze, the colour from his face draining away as his eyes met a horrific scene.

Only a few metres away from where he was sitting stood Amanda Obereen. And Charlie Cox. He was pushing her against the wall, grinding into her, trying to kiss those pretty lips Dimitri had once had possession over. She kept pushing at Charlie, refusing his kisses. She looked like she was about to cry. "Charlie, stop," she begged but he would not listen.

An anger like he had never felt before scorched his veins. What does Charlie Cox think he's doing with my girl? That thought was all it took for Dimitri to pull himself up from the couch and race towards the pair.

He laid a rough hand on Charlie's shoulder and shoved him back, putting all the hate he had for the boy into that shove. "Didn't you hear the lady, Cox? She told you to stop."

Charlie looked up and his eyes hardened once they met Dimitri's eyes. "She broke up with you for a reason. Now do us a both a favour and get lost, arsehole," Charlie sneered.

Amanda coughed. "How about you go get us some punch, Charles? I want to have another word with my ex," she said. The way she said it seemed as if Dimitri was desperate and would not stop bugging Amanda which was not true at all because they had not even so much as said a word to each other after their break up. Was she really a bitch? Dimitri refused to believe so.

Charlie Cox looked between Amanda and Dimitri and shrugged as if to say, 'oh well, my job is done.' He then sighed and did as Amanda instructed him, trudging to the food table.

"I told you to stay away," Amanda said once Charlie was out of earshot. "Why do you want to make this so hard?"

Dimitri looked at her and his eyes flashed with anger but now for a entirely different reason and directed to a different person. "You're unbelievable," he spat as he gave her a look of disbelief.

Amanda sighed tiredly and leaned back against the wall. "Dimitri," she said and the way she said his name sent a pang of longing at his heart. "We broke up. That's it. Why don't you just make this easy and leave me alone. I don't like you anymore," she said but her tone of voice and emotion playing in her eyes betrayed her words.

"I, more than anyone, know that that's not true."

Amanda's eyes flashed as she looked back at him. He knew he was making this hard for her but it was not like he was making this any easier for him.

"When did you become to arrogant?" she said, her tone turning accusing.

"I'm not arrogant. I'm just stating the true, cold hard facts," he replied curtly, the anger in his system growing stronger by the second.

"I don't like you anymore. We are not together. I bloody broke up with you. Now leave me the hell alone," she snapped and walked away from Dimitri and towards Charlie. As if to prove a point, she leaned on her tiptoes and wound her arms around Charlie's neck, kissing his lips fervently.

Just like she had once done to him.

He needed Juniper.

Juniper Stauff was beyond drunk. She had come over to the bartender and ordered something strong thinking that she wanted to get this heavy feeling in her heart off. She was not going to last long and she wanted to own everything she wanted.

In a daze she tried counting the empty solo cups that she poured into her mouth. She gave up counting after number eleven. What was he number that followed after eleven? She couldn't remember and for unknown reasons that irked her. She started counting from again all over again as she thought that if she started afresh she would remember the number that came after eleven. But she fell silent after she counted the eleventh cup and let out a frustrated sigh. What was the bloody number?

She turned to the bartender and put a smile to her lips. "One more," she slurred putting a hand up thinking that she was in a classroom and the bartender was her teacher and that the only way she could attain his attention was if she raised her hand like one would do in a classroom. She had no idea how absurd and silly she looked amongst the crowd.

The bartender ignored her feeling a little guilty that he had supplied the little girl with too much alcohol. "Yo hottie," she snapped rudely at the bartender. When he looked at her, she blushed and giggled. Now that she had thought about it he was pretty hot. "One more," she said, her eyes half-lidded as she leaned across the table.

"No," he replied, "I suggest you go look for your boyfriend and ask him to drive you home."

She frowned, her face turning into a funny expression. "That would be lovely except I don't have a boyfriend. I do, however, have eyes on this one guy. He's a total hottie," she gushed. "His name is Dimitri. And his name is so drool-worthy. Don't you think?"

The bartender definitely felt awkward. "Uh yeah," he said. "Why don't you just ask this boy out?"

Juniper sighed dramatically. "You see, that's the problem. Him and Amanda, his ex, recently broke up. He's still hung over her and it sucks arse if I'm being entirely honest. I even dressed up for him! He just won't notice me," she complained.

She had no idea where all of this was coming from and why she was telling this all to the bartender, a stranger, a person who she was no idea about. Maybe it was because she was feeling slightly dizzy and dazed. But, truthfully, it felt nice to talk to someone about it. Even though that person was a stranger and she was in a drunken state.

"Well, the night is young," the bartender said. He no more wanted her at the table getting any more drunk than she already was. He wanted to get rid of her. "I bet he's in the crowd," he said pointing to the dance floor. "Make him notice you."

Juniper gasped and looked at the bartender in amazement. "Wow!" she exclaimed, "you're a genius."

"Yes, I am. Now shoo. Go make this Dimitri boy yours."

"I sure will," Juniper winked, her lips turning up into a smile before she turned around and headed towards the dance floor.

Once her feet touched the dance floor, however, the music consumed and she began to dance wildly with the crowd. Dimitri has slipped her mind so quickly.

"You look stunning," a husky voice entered her ear and the proximity sent shivers down her spine.

She whirled around looking for the face of the voice. "Thank you," she smiled when her eyes met a sandy haired boy. "You look stunning yourself."

The boy pretended he could not hear what she was saying. "Sorry?" he shouted, "what was that you just said?"

"I said you look stunning," she shouted back not aware that now that boy had placed his hand on her waist.

His head dropped low and his mouth grazed her ear. "Lets say we take this conversation upstairs? The music is too loud and I can't hear you," the boy said. He pulled back his head waiting for a response as a mischievous glint shone clear in his eyes.

She nodded innocently not aware of what this boy's intention was. He smirked and took her hand as he lead her up the stairs. Once they found a room, the boy slowly pushed her towards the bed.

They stood by the bed, the back of Juniper's knees pressing against it. The boy hovered above her. She stared intently into his eyes, her own eyes full of wonder. "Your eyes are so blue," she whispered.

"Yeah?" he smirked as he gave her shoulders a shove which resulted her to fall back on the bed.

She frowned, hurt that he pushed her so very urgently. "Why'd you do that?" she inquired, a little angry mask taking its place on her face.

He got onto the bed and crawled towards her, his hand gliding up her bare legs. She giggled. It felt ticklish. "Stop," she said in between a giggle.

He leaned over her, one of his legs between hers, his face only inches away. He then buried his head into the nape of her neck and began to tug her dress up. She gasped, her expression morphing into one of that of horror as his cold lips pressed against her collarbone and sent a wave of shivers down her spine.

She pushed at his chest but he would not bulge. "Stop," she begged less happily this time. His hand had travelled up her dress and he had begun to tug at her underwear. "Stop," she whimpered trying to get out of his hold.

His hands gripped her wrists and pulled them over her head. He looked down at her and his eyes glinted with lust. "Please stop," Juniper sobbed.

"Trust me, love," he said leaning over her petite body so that the stale smell of alcohol from his breath washed over her face. "Once I start, you'd beg me not to stop."

She screamed in frustration before she let out a throaty sob that signalled defeat. "Stop it, you arsehole," she yelled as she thrashed against the boy's hold. "Please...stop it."

The door swung open and someone had come to her rescue. "Hey!" a familiar voice shouted. "Who the fuck do you think you are? What the hell do you think you're doing with my best friend?"

Juniper was sure that she heard a groan and a smack, followed by a punch and she was almost certain that someone was getting beat up. But at that moment nothing but her exposure mattered and she curled into a ball and sobbed uncontrollably.

A few moments had passed before she felt a pair of warm arms tighten around her and she welcomed the familiar embrace as she found warmth and comfort in those arms. The pair of arms helped her get off the bed and stand on her two feet. She leaned towards the body, unable to find her centre of mass. And then she felt everything rise to her throat and in and instant she was bent over. She vomited, spewing her guts on the floor.

"This night cannot possibly get anymore worse," the owner of the strong pair of arms groaned. Two seconds later she returned back to the warm arms. And then she cried and cried as the warm arms carried her out of the room, out of the door, out of the havoc and into the open, fresh air.

Then she had finally blacked out.

Chapter 6

Juniper Stauff tossed and turned in bed. The bed was rough, the pillow was stiff and the blanket was not as soft as it usually was. She breathed in the scent of Dimitri's cologne and smiled in content. Then she realised that this was not her bed. Her pillow surely didn't have Dimitri's fragrance on it. Her eyes opened and she jolted awake, sitting upright, her senses alert.

Instantly her head began to pound and Juniper winced at the throbbing pain in her head. Looking around the room she realised that only a two nights ago she was here. This was Dimitri's room.

But how did she get here? She could not even remember anything from last night. The last she remembered was her going over to the bartender at Brooke's party and drinking away into the night. For some odd reason the number eleven popped into her mind. That confused her. Why was she thinking about the number eleven?

Then something else struck her. She wasn't wearing the dress she attended Brooke's party in. Instead she was wearing a long, baggy blue shirt and chequered boxers. The last she checked, the shirt and the boxers were not part of her closet. She remembered the blue shirt on Dimitri...but the boxers? Was it his too? Oh gosh, Juniper thought while blushing at the same time. Why was she wearing his boxers and how on earth did she get into these clothes?

Flustered by the thought of Dimitri getting a look at her body, she got up and walked towards the door. Once out of the room and pass the door, she heard muffled voices emerge from downstairs. Maybe Dimitri was watching television.

Wait. What if his father was home? Juniper was intimidated by Mr Remirez. Before his wife's disappearance, he was always jolly and she loved how Mr Remirez treated her as his own daughter. But after his wife's disappearance he never gave Juniper a second glance and when she tried to talk to him or offer her condolences, he would grunt and push her away, swearing at her. Dimitri would then apologize for his father's ruthless behaviour and he made sure that Juniper kept her distance from Mr Remirez.

Juniper Stauff leaned against the doorway of the living room. Dimitri sat on the sofa, one leg on the coffee table as he watched reruns of Sherlock on the BBC channel. Juniper smiled once she saw him. Only if she could make him hers.

Juniper cleared her throat, the throbbing in her head slightly lessened. "Good morning, Dimmy," she greeted.

"Definitely not a good morning, is it?" Dimitri asked, eyebrows raised jokingly.

"Definitely not. Hey, listen, do you have anything to make this headache go away?"

"Oh yes!" he said. "Give me a sec." He disappeared into the kitchen and a minute later he returned with a glass of milk in one hand and two tablets in the other hand.

She looked at the medication, eyeing the pair of tablets wearily. "It's aspirin, June," Dimitri said, reassuringly when he saw her expression. "Swallow it down with the milk. It'll help ease the pain."

Juniper found a seat on the sofa and Dimitri followed her, taking a seat beside her. She took his advice and swallowed down the two tablets of aspirin by drinking it down with the milk. Juniper shut her eyes, willing the pain to go away but it still throbbed very violently in her head. After a few minutes, her head throbbed less and she let out a breath of relief. She thought she was going to endure the horrible headache forever - at that moment it had seemed so.

Her head felt much lighter and clearer. However, the events of last night were still forgotten. "You wouldn't happen to know what happened to me last night, would you?" she asked curiously as she tilted her head so she could look up at Dimitri.

He returned her stare and she saw deep concern in his expression. "You don't remember anything?" When Juniper shook her head, he had added, "at all?"

"I remember the number eleven."

He rolled his eyes at her. Then he frowned. "You were really drunk last night then." He looked a bit hesitant before he told her the happenings of last night, omitting a few details. "There was this guy who wanted to take advantage of you. I was looking for you and when I passed the room you two were in I heard shouts and cries. I didn't know it was you until I opened the door. I've never heard you cry before."

"Surprise surprise," she said weakly. "Juniper cries. Shocker? I think so."

He frowned at her response. He was positive that something was wrong with her. His best friend had never acted like this before so why was she acting like this now? He was sure that something had happened.

The only reason he went to the party the previous night was because his father was not at home for dinner. Mr Remirez some-times did that. He would not come home for dinner and Dimitri would not see him for the next two days. He didn't know what his father was up to. It was a great, big world and if Dimitri was being entirely honest with himself, he was scared of the world's greatness. He might hate who his father has become but he still cared for Mr Remirez and still loved him because deep down the man that Dimitri loved and had the pleasure of calling dad still thrived. That man was just buried too deep in to escape. Dimitri definitely did not want his father to take the path his uncle, Miles Miller, followed.

"I feel so violated," Juniper whispered so low, Dimitri almost missed out on her words. She played with her fingers, her dark hair cascading forward and covering her face, hiding it from view. She looked lost and Dimitri's heart clenched when he looked at Juniper in such a broken state. He'd never seen her upset.

"June," he said softly and she looked up at him at the mention of her nickname. "If there's anything you want to talk about or get off your chest you know I am here for you, right?"

A small, sad smile touched her pink lips. "Likewise, Dimmy," she said. He furrowed his brows when he heard her reply. Did he think what Juniper meant or...? "I'm not that stupid," she added and Dimitri was struck by a slight spasm of panic. What did she know?

"Anywho," she said this time smiling wide, clearing all the dense atmosphere. "How did I get into these clothes?"

The second those words left her mouth a blush rose to his face. "Oh," he stuttered. "I might have, um, you know..."

She feigned anger and tried not to laugh. He was so gullible sometimes. "You took a look at my goodies?"

"Well, I wasn't going to let you sleep so uncomfortably!" he defended, his face growing redder.

Juniper giggled at Dimitri's response but he didn't miss the pink that now tainted her cheeks. "It's okay, Dimmy," she said shaking her head while laughing. He was just too cute.

Then she froze. "Shit," she said, her expression turning sour. "My parents. I am so dead."

Dimitri was the one laughing this time. "So much for curfew."

"Hey!" she fumed, slouching into the couch and crossing her arms over her chest. Dimitri smiled. Her personality compared to no other human being; he admired her quite a lot.

Juniper didn't like it when someone witnessed her in a sad mood, Dimitri noticed. What he saw last night - the way Eric Sander was violating his best friend - that lit a fire within him. It was the spark that let the bomb off. All the anger that consumed Dimitri was let out into the punches and kicks he gave Eric Sander. After he almost beat Eric Sander to the pulp he had felt guilty. But now, sitting with Juniper, he realised that Eric Sander deserved what he got. Nobody could dare lay a dangerous finger on Juniper Stauff.

However, what happened with Amanda was out of his control and no more his concern but that didn't mean that he was not hurt.

He was hurt and sad. Most of all, Dimitri felt anger. It was Amanda he decided to open up to. It was Amanda that he chose to show his demons to. It was Amanda whom he loved. And what did she do? In return, she threw all that away from the sake of popularity; for the sake of her high school career. The fact that Dimitri knew that Amanda loved him back but was too afraid to say it because then she would no more have a social life, friends or popularity was was angered him the most. Amanda didn't stand up for what she thought was right. No, she caved into peer pressure and followed the crowd into it's stereotypical - and very superficial, in Dimitri's head - path.

Juniper, who knew by just the look on Dimitri's face, could tell that something was bothering him. She slid closer to him and nudged him with her elbow, trying to push out the thought of Dimitri actually getting a glimpse at her body. Oh God. "Yo Dimmy," she said waving her hand in front of his blank stare.

"Huh?" he asked as he turned his attention back to Juniper.

"What's up?"

"You mean other than me running into my ex or you having a horrible night? Nothing much." Dimitri feared to tell Juniper what really happened last night. Yes, he told her that Eric Sander tried to take advantage of her but he didn't want her to actually know just how much Eric violated her to the extent that she broke down, something Juniper had never done in public nor in front of her best friend. It hurt Dimitri to see his best-friend like that. He couldn't even imagine what she would feel. Of course, by the end of the day or the next day she would remember everything but hopefully it wouldn't have the same effect. He had never seen Juniper sad and now that he had he hated the sight of it.

Juniper rolled her eyes at Dimitri's response. "C'mon," she said, "it doesn't take a genius to see that there's something obviously bothering you."

He sighed. Usually he would tell Amanda what his problems were but now the problem revolved around her. Juniper reached for his hand and squeezed it encouragingly, crinkles appearing at the ends of her eyes as she smiled. "Look, if you don't want to talk about it then okay. We can just sit here and watch Sherlock because you know how much I love this show. And I'll worry about my parents later."

Dimitri looked sideways at her. Even in a moment like this she seemed to be happy. But now Dimitri knew not to judge her by how she looked and the facial expression that she wore. Ever since she pulled out that revenge card he seemed to be looking at her more clearly and he analysed her every move. She was hiding something from him. Dimitri could tell that Juniper had a façade up. But was there a reason behind putting up a façade? Was there a reason why she wore a mask from her own best friend?

"It's Amanda," he said after a pregnant pause.

Of course Juniper knew this and suddenly the whole reason of going to the party returned to her. She only hoped that Charlie Cox played a convincing scene. "Oh," she said. "Did you run into Mandy last night?"

His hold on Juniper's hand tightened. "Yeah," he said in a hushed tone. "She's hooking up with Charlie."

Juniper stayed silent. His eyes looked glassy and he was squeezing her hand with so much force due to his anger that she could almost see the veins flow up his arm clearly. He was hurt and furious, that much Juniper could tell.

"I just don't get why she's so stupid," he said, his jaw clenching.

"So," Juniper said, softly, her tone suggestive. "What are you going to do?"

Dimitri faced her. "I want to know what your scheme is. This whole revenge plan of yours."

She was startled by his sudden approach but she'd be lying if she said she didn't feel the least bit content at his statement. "Why?" she inquired.

"I'm considering taking you up on that...favour," he said, adding the last but uncertainly. Juniper tried her best to hide her smile. "Are you sure? Because this time once you're in, you can't back out."

Dimitri Remirez looked at Juniper Stauff. A flicker of doubt passed through him when he thought of his love for Amanda but that was soon replaced by anger when he remembered the compromising position she found him and what she had done to him, leaving him in such a horrific state.

His features turned hard as he nodded and thought to himself that what he was about to do was at least 99% right. "Yes," he said after mulling over Juniper's proposal. "I'm all in."

CHAPTER 7

J uniper Stauff and Dimitri Remirez knelt behind the big 4x4 jeep that lay in the driveway of Amanda Obereen's house. Juniper was excited but Dimitri was nervous as hell. "June, this is a stupid idea," Dimitri said, pulling at the sleeve of Juniper's shirt to get her attention.

They were both dressed in black and Juniper insisted on the ski masks. She said that it would make them look more subtle and would blend into the starry, dark night. We look more like robbers, Dimitri thought.

Juniper sighed as she looked up at him, craning her neck so she could get a view of him. Then she remembered that she couldn't exactly see his face. "Not with this again," she said. "You said you were in, Dimmy. You can't back out now, especially since we're already here! Why are you so indecisive?"

"I just," he said, searching for the right words. "If she gets hurt..."

"Look, you trust me. Right?"

"Of course, I trust you. I wouldn't have told you the thing that embarrasses her the most if I didn't trust you." Dimitri couldn't lie to himself. He was excited to see the hurt expression on Amanda's face, to get payback, except he couldn't really bear to see her hurt. He could feel at the pit of his stomach that this wasn't right.

Juniper slipped her hands into his and tugged him closer, whispering as if someone would overhear them in the dead of the night. "She hurt you and it pains me to see you this broken over such a worthless girl. If she truly did love you the she would have stayed with her Prince Charming."

A sudden fire blazed in Dimitri's eyes and he yanked his hand from her grasp. "She does love me," he hissed.

"Maybe she does. But you're hurt because she chose her friends over you."

Dimitri's anger washed out in an instant. It was no use fighting with Juniper. "Why do you care so much?" he asked, his eyes searching for an answer.

She gave him a blank, pointed look. "That's the stupidest question you've ever asked and I've ever heard. You're my best friend, Dimmy. Of course I care for you."

Dimitri nodded but because he knew Juniper so well, he knew she was not telling him something. And something else within him knew that it was better off not knowing. After all, he's known for a few days now that she wasn't telling him something important.

"The back door," Dimitri said at last, helping Juniper to her feet so that they were both standing. "We get in through the back door."

Juniper nodded. If only he knew just how much she liked him. But would the knowledge of her feelings change his mind and deter his emotions? Probably not, Juniper thought.

He was still hung over Amanda. Juniper couldn't really blame him for loving Amanda. Amanda was smart, funny, adorable, hot and everything Dimitri Remirez wanted. Frankly, Juniper was not what Dimitri wanted. Maybe he saw Juniper as a friend he felt overly protective over or maybe like his younger sister. But she so badly wanted him to see her as more than just as friend - as girlfriend material. Too bad he doesn't, Juniper thought in an attempt to cheer herself up, he doesn't know what he's missing out on.

They walked across the lawn, creeping to the back door slowly and carefully so that they didn't step or trip over anything that would cause unnecessary noise. When they got to the backdoor Dimitri paused and fished out a key from his back pocket.

Juniper was surprised. In all honesty she didn't think that the back door would be locked or if it was then she thought the key would be hidden under a mat or something of the sort. She didn't expect Dimitri to have a spare key to the back door of the Obereen's household amongst his possessions.

"You have a key," she state the obvious, shock lacing itself delicately through her voice.

Dimitri peeked at her through his ski mask and looked at his best friend's blue, dazzling eyes. "Yeah, I do. I used to come over sometimes," he said, stumbling over his words a little and Juniper could almost picture the embarrassed look beneath his ski mask; his face burning red. "June, are the ski masks really necessary?"

"Absolutely," she said, her lips lifting into an amused smile. Then she remembered that Dimitri could not see her face so she rolled her eyes. "Okay, enough with the stalling. Now, tell me why we're going through the back door?"

"Well, it's not a secret that the Obereen's are loaded. They have a security alarm and the alarm is only activated through the front door and a few other specific places. That's why we're using the back door," he explained briefly as he fitted the key into the keyhole and opened the door. "After you, milady," he grinned giving a short bow.

Juniper rolled her eyes at his gesture and tried to stifle her laughter. She stepped inside and felt her cheeks heat up as she thought about his gesture. She had it bad for Dimitri Remirez that she even went to such lengths to get him. She should have known that the truest of things was not attainable with a twisted mind.

The backdoor led to the kitchen. The kitchen wasn't all that fancy but Juniper knew if she had this extravagant kitchen - especially that lovely oven -- she would want to bake and cook all day.

They tiptoed around the counter in the kitchen and Dimitri led the way upstairs. As they made their way up the staircase Juniper couldn't help but admire the beautiful house. She could only dream to live in a house this vast and lovely. When they passed the dining room and living room she almost dropped her mouth. The dining room was well furnished and had dim brown walls. Over the table - which from at first glance looked like it was made of mahogany - on the ceiling hung a low, big chandelier which Juniper was sure that if she switched it on, it would light up the hold room so she could observe it even more clearly. She was tempted to do just that but lucky enough Dimitri pulled her away.

When they reached Amanda's room Dimitri laid a hesitant hand on the doorknob and almost immediately retreated his hand as if the doorknob had burned his hand. Juniper looked up at him and her expression softened. She gave him an encouraging smile before she remembered that he couldn't see her face through the ski mask. "Should I?" she offered.

He nodded. "Do you have the bag?" he asked, silently hoping that Juniper took the right bag from his car.

"Yup," she said holding up the black bag for him to see. It had a stale smell and that was what told Dimitri that she picked up the right bag. Juniper might have had a plan but Dimitri was plotting as well and he was going to make sure that by the end of that night Charlie Cox would not go unpunished.

She twisted the door knob and opened the door. They both stepped into Amanda's room and Juniper took a while to adjust herself to the room. Juniper was immediately awed by the sight that greeted her eyes. The room was twice as big as Juniper's. The walls were painted a faint orange which gave her a sense of calm despite the darkness that shrouded them. There was a dressing table at one corner of the room which had make-up all over it with an oval mirror that hung directly above it on the wall. There was a study table which had books piled up neatly in a stack. A few feet away from the study table was a double sized bed in which Amanda's petite body laid in, peacefully and deep in sleep.

Juniper looked sideways and saw Dimitri staring at Amanda with a longing look in his eyes. She turned away and closed her own eyes as she tried to subside the twisted feeling in her heart. She so looked that he could looked at her that way. "Come on," she finally said. "Let's get this over with."

Dimitri returned back to reality as he took the bag from Juniper. He quickly untied it and opened her undergarment drawer.

"Wait," Juniper said. "Are you really going to put tuna in her bras and panties?" She almost forgot that Dimitri had been going out with Amanda for the last nine months.

Dimitri looked back at Juniper through his ski mask. Well, to say the moment was tensed and awkward would be stating the obvious. He shrugged before saying, "knowing Amanda she probably has another stack of clothes stacked somewhere else. She would never afford to miss a day of school. She loves fashion and clothes so she definitely has a secret closet somewhere in this house. I may have dated her for a long time and been in this house a lot but that doesn't mean I would look for this closet. I used my time to-"

"Yeah, make out with her," waving his explanation off that was drifting off too far for her to handle anymore.

"Putting tuna in her undergarments is the perfect solution. She'd have to choice but to come to school smelling like tuna."

Juniper nodded, a little flustered at the detailed information. "Good thinking," was all she mustered to say.

Dimitri turned away from Juniper and pulled out a box before dumping the contents of the bag into the Amanda's undergarments drawer with his gloved hands. One of the perks of taking revenge at Amanda at this time of the night was that she was such a heavy sleeper that she was often completely oblivious to the things around her.

Juniper then picked up the box that Dimitri pulled out of the bag and opened it. She grabbed three eggs from the box while Dimitri took the other three eggs. They both approached Amanda's bed and they stood either side of her head. Juniper looked at her partner in crime and when he nodded she cracked the first egg open and the goo of white and yellow spilled from the shell and coated Amanda's curly black hair. After she was done with her three eggs, she instructed Dimitri to hand over his three eggs and when all six eggs were finally done cracking and coated Amanda's hair, they packed the eggs and box back in the bag and headed for Amanda's door.

They stepped outside the door of Amanda's room and Juniper made the mistake of tripping over Dimitri's foot which had resulted them to topple over which thereby caused a disruption in the silence.

Instinct told them to freeze. Dimitri had his arms wound around Juniper and it looked as if he was almost on top on her. The proximity between their faces didn't faze Dimitri but Juniper had an overwhelming feeling to pull Dimitri closer and kiss him full on the lips. No, she thought, not yet.

Dimitri shook his head slowly which told her not to move and they stayed still in the same position for about a minute or so. Then he nodded. "Phew," he sighed as he lifted himself off the ground and off Juniper.

He stood up and then helped his best friend onto her feet. "You okay?" he asked, concern lacing his voice. "I didn't crush you, did I?"

"Maybe a little," she teased in a hushed voice. "I just want to get the hell out of here."

After this little incident that left her flushed she had forgotten the reason as to why they took the backdoor and not the front door when they entered the house. She stalked downstairs, past the dining room and living room - too much in a rush to admire the rooms again - and put her hand on the door knob of the front door.

"No!" Dimitri exclaimed but it was of no use for it was all too late.

Juniper Stauff had already opened the door and a second later the security system was alerted which set the alarm off as it wailed in the silence.

Juniper whirled around to face Dimitri and both the teenagers shared a panicked look in their eyes. "Oh shit," they said in unison.

CHAPTER 8

Juniper Stuaff and Dimitri Remirez froze yet again for the second time that night. Panic swelled from the depths of their chests until Dimitri's panic toned down and he returned back to reality. "June, stop standing there like a statue. Run!"

Dimitri didn't realise that he had shouted until Juniper looked at him with an even heightened panic look. Oh God, why did the universe have to be against them at that moment?

"Dimitri?" came Mr Obereen's voice from upstairs. "Is that you?" He sounded angry. There were numerous nights when Mr Obereen found his daughter spending the night with Dimitri in her bedroom. He didn't exactly despise Dimitri but he didn't like the boy much either. He certainly did look down upon the relationship that his daughter and Dimitri shared.

"Fuck," Dimitri cursed under his breath before he grabbed Juniper's hand and yanked her out the door. Together they ran across the lawn, past Mr Obereen's 4X4 and safely across the road with Juniper stumbling after.

They got into Dimitri's car and hurriedly he slid the key into the ignition but when he turned on it the car would not start up. "Shit. Not now," he cried as he kept at his attempts to revive the car back from the dead.

Mr Obereen had appeared on his lawn, a cricket bat in his right hand and his dark, chubby face was burning red with anger. Mrs Obereen arrived shortly after her husband and unlike her husband, she didn't appear to be angry but scared. Maybe she thought that they were being robbed and that Dimitri and Juniper were the robbers. It didn't help Juniper's and Dimitri's case since they were the ones who were in ski masks and, indeed, resembled robbers perfectly.

That thought was thrown out Dimitri's head when his car roared back to life. "Yes!" he exclaimed, victory evident in his voice as the car had finally started.

"Go, go, go!" Juniper pumped as a means for urging him to drive faster.

Once they were three blocks away from the Obereen household Juniper and Dimitri calmed down. They had both taken off their ski masks. Juniper relaxed and sunk back into her seat. She closed her eyes and a little smile played at her lips. She couldn't believe she just broke into someone's house and got away with it. That night went better than expected, she had thought and she began to hum. What she didn't know was that she got her hopes up too high only to have them crushed after her fair share of happiness.

"That tune," Dimitri said, "I've heard it before."

"The Hanging Tree," Juniper replied as she opened her eyes and beamed up at Dimitri. "So, Dimmy, it's pretty late but I know this amazing place that serve coffee and it's open 24/7 so how ab-hey! Where are you going?"

In the middle of Juniper's speech he took an abrupt turn making Juniper stumble over her words.

"I went along with this crazy plan of yours because you were certain that revenge is justice. And I guess I'm accepting that now. But it's not fair on behalf of vengeance if revenge is only taken on the half part of it," Dimitri said, determination lacing his voice.

Juniper scrunched her brows. "What on earth are you talking about?"

Dimitri looked at Juniper. She was a little startled at the fiery look in his eyes. It gave him a sinister look and while he did look hot - Juniper couldn't deny that face - it gave her the creeps.

"Well, we only completed half of our - or my - revenge. We took revenge on Mandy but wasn't Charlie part of this, too?" he mused deliberately making the wheel in Juniper's head turn.

They way he was speaking made Juniper's heart drop. No, she thought. She made a deal with Charlie - she can't go back on her word. "Look," she said, "whatever you're thinking; no. Let's not be so rash-"

"I have the right to take my revenge. He stole my girl."

No, this is not how it's supposed to go, thought Juniper. "Dimitri, this is absolutely ludicrous-"

"Using big words won't change my mind, June."

"Dimmy, he didn't do anything to you," Juniper said as she hoped somehow the car would magically turn around. She couldn't go ahead with this.

Dimitri's eyes flashed as he parked the car across the street of the Cox's household and turned to face her. "He didn't do anything?" boomed Dimitri. "If I didn't know any better, I'd say you're defending him. Or protecting him. Whatever it is, you're against this amazing idea of mine for a reason."

She forced a laugh hoping that it would brush off the nervousness that she was feeling. "Okay, now that's definitely ludicrous. I just don't want to get in Charlie's way. He didn't do anything to me-"

"Oh," he said, the tone of his voice clipped. "And Mandy did?"

Juniper paled at his words. How was she to respond to that? Amanda stole the love of her life. Then she crushed the heart of the aforementioned person. That only infuriated her more and her hatred for Amanda Obereen grew even though she may have been the cause of their breakup. "No," she finally croaked, "but she hurt you."

Dimitri let out a hopeless sigh and laid his head back on the seat. His eyes closed and Juniper watched his body tense up as he spoke. It kind of broke her that Dimitri was head over heels - sneakers, in this case - over such a stupid girl. If Amanda truly did love Dimitri - as he did she - then why did she break his heart? Why did she leave him? Why did she let go?

"You don't get it, do you?" Dimitri said as he ran a hand through his tousled hair. He looked devastatingly handsome when he did that. "Put yourself in my shoes, June. How would it feel if the love of your life cheated on you with the person you hated the most? I used to be physically bullied by Charlie. After Amanda became my girlfriend the physical bullying stopped. But the emotional one didn't. It was always Charlie Cox who touched on the subjects that pushed my buttons. He teased me about Mum leaving and Dad being so detached and unfriendly. He teased me and mocked me and labelled me as gay and a prick and fucking loner." Juniper's heart was shattering. "But you've always been there for me even though most of the time I closed myself up and kept myself in that uncrackable shell of mine. You've always stuck by me and these past nine months Amanda has."

Juniper's heart clenched at his words and she did her best to suppress a frown. She leaned across Dimitri's car and linked her hands with his, entwining her fingers with his before she gave his hand a squeeze and offered him an encouraging smile. A smile that was filled with light and hope. But the darkness in her soul had already sunk too deep to leave. Nobody was aware of that - how could they when she held up the perfect façade? - at that moment and not even she did. Juniper was suffering but why she was avoiding talking to her parents about her suffering was a mystery. She just wanted to live a happy and carefree life but how was she going to do that without facing her problems?

Dimitri didn't look back at Juniper nor did he acknowledge her encouragement. He simply stared out the window, a broken and furious expression gracing his delicate features. "That day, when I saw my girlfriend and my bully in the janitor's closet, I lost it. Seeing Amanda and Charlie kiss like there was no tomorrow...it broke something in me. I could practically hear my heart shatter-ing. I've gone through enough emotional trauma to know that I should never get my hopes up high. But I was stupid and like the fool my father calls me, I fell into Amanda's trap. And Charlie. The way he was handling my girl in that closet... I could have ripped his head from his body, removed every vital organ from his body and feed him to the pigs. Except I have no chance against Charlie Cox. And in that moment I was shocked. It was only later, when my mind finally started to accept the fact that Mandy broke up with me did I realise how betrayed Mandy had left me and how infuriated Charlie had left me."

Even though Juniper never really did experience the emotions that Dimitri had, the way he spoke was enough to scare her and she was left hollow after his little speech. Maybe Dimitri did deserve revenge on Charlie. But she had made a promise. Juniper Stauff never broke a promise.

"I'm sorry," she finally said, her voice small compared to Dimitri's recently booming voice.

He looked at her this time. "I don't expect you to understand."

"But I kind of do," she said and she wasn't entirely lying. "But Dimmy, you're too emotional now. Your head is not clear and you're being-"

"Rash?" Dimitri finished for her. "Well, I don't give a flying fuck right now. You can't do anything. You can't stop me. So whether you're with me on this or not I'm going to do what I came here to do."

Juniper's heart dropped.

"And all I need is my phone and this bag," Dimitri said as he leaned over and pulled a different black bag from the back seat.

Juniper raised her brows. "What?" Juniper asked, confused. "Black bag. I thought-"

"This one's for Charlie Cox, packed specially by me. It has shaving cream and a big fuzzy teddy bear. All I need is my phone," Dimitri finished with a smirk.

"A phone which has a camera," Juniper whispered, the anxiousness slowly building up in her stomach as realisation dawned her.

She knew exactly what he was going to do. Taking a deep breath, she nodded. "Okay."

"Okay?" he quirked his brows.

"Okay, I'm in," she said as she struggled to smile to make it sound convincing. "What are we waiting here for?"

Dimitri grinned. "Great!" he exclaimed. "Revenge, part two, here we come!"

It was a good thing Charlie Cox's house was not a double story one. Dimitri Remirez and Juniper Stauff easily got into Charlie's room through the window. It was July - one of the hottest times in Sereneigo. It was no surprise that Charlie kept the window open to let at least some air in to cool the warm atmosphere inside his room.

Despite being the bad boy of the school Charlie wasn't so financially stable. He was not even emotionally stable. Juniper knew his troubles and what put him in the distress that caught up with him. No, she thought, this is wrong.

But she couldn't stop now, could she? Not when she was so very close to having Dimitri's heart. But even the oh-so-wise Juniper Stauff never saw her fate. And her fate held terrible things in store for her mixed among the wonderful things.

"Shh," Dimitri warned when Juniper unzipped the black bag. "Hand me the teddy bear."

Juniper looked at Dimitri's face with a pained look upon her own. "Juniper," he said, his voice holding an unfriendly tone. But it was laced with the tone of desperation and she felt her heart twist. She sighed and reluctantly handed the teddy bear over to Dimitri.

He then, in turn, silently and carefully fitted the teddy bear into Charlie's arms. Charlie stirred and Dimitri froze, his eyes widening silently and both Juniper and Dimitri held their breaths. Then Charlie squeezed the teddy bear, pulling it closer towards his chest as a smile slowly made its way to his chapped lips.

Seeing Charlie in this state made Juniper sympathise with him. She couldn't do this to him. After everything he went through - with almost losing a brother after he lost his father - Juniper couldn't do this to him. It was a simple question of would she or would she not?

Dimitri fished out his phone and began snapping pictures of Charlie, taking each photo with a new angle. Once he was done he smirked as he muttered under his breath, "who is the gay one now, Cox?"

He looked satisfied which was the opposite of what Juniper felt. He turned to Juniper and for the first time in years she frowned down upon his actions. She'd never witnessed this side of him; it was dark and unattractive and she momentarily found herself questioning in where her heart lay.

"The shaving cream," Dimitri requested and held out his hand.

Juniper looked up at him, her blue eyes dazzling with conflicting emotions. "Don't you think it's enough?' she tried to reason.

Dimitri did not give her a reply. He simply continued to hold out his hand. Gritting her teeth together to prevent her from swearing him, she pulled the bottle of shaving cream from the bag and put in down harshly into Dimitri's hand.

He continued with his work by outlining Charlie's face with shaving cream. Charlie must have felt something because the next thing that happened was that his hand came up and brushed at the shaving cream annoyingly. Then he put his thumb into his thumb and proceeded to suck it, his face looking relieved as he hugged the teddy bear tighter against his naked chest.

Dimitri smirked. "Perfect. This is going better than I thought it would." He then proceeded to take more pictures of a silly, baby-faced-looking Charlie Cox. "Done!" he said at last, putting his phone back into his pocket. A victorious smile played at his lips and while that smile did make him look cute, Juniper found it rather disgusting and that surprised her. Nothing Dimitri had done in the past had disgusted her so why did it now, in Charlie's room?

"You go ahead," she said, forcing a smile to her very own lips. "I'll follow you in a minute."

Dimitri nodded, not doubting his best friend's actions as he headed out the window. Once he was out the window, Juniper swerved around and walked towards Charlie's study table looking for a piece of paper so she could leave a note, addressing Charlie and telling him how sorry she was for what was about to smack him in the face the following morning. Instead of finding the piece of plain paper that she was seeking, she stumbled upon a letter addressed to Charlie Cox from Jeremy Cox.

Seeing the name Jeremy Cox brought tears to her eyes and a lump rose up to her throat. She could almost visualize what happened three years ago. No, she thought shaking her head as the images from three years ago flickered to her mind. She had buried that incident deep down and she was too afraid to awaken the memory.

Picking up the envelope with shaking hands, her fingers glazed over the rough exterior. Her heart accelerated and curiosity started to nibble and eat away inside her stomach. Finally giving into the curiosity she quickly pulled out the letter from the worn out envelope. Her eyes scanned the words and the lump in her throat grew bigger.

Hey Charles,

I've been dying for the 30th of August. It's only a few days away but I reckon when you receive this letter I'll probably be released the next day or so. They say I'm better and I'm doing well. They keep saying that though and it gets tiring hearing that over and over and over and over again. I know I'm better. I don't need their words to reassure me.

Obviously I always sneak a cig when I can. Trading cigarettes is fun here if I'm being honest but I've already told you that in my past letters. I don't know how else I would've survived here if it weren't for smoking and I bet mum will beat my arse when I come back home. She always hated my smoking habit.

Anyway, I think I'm glad that I didn't try to escape rehab after my failed attempt. What I did three years ago, Charles... Forget it, okay? I was an idiot. And I was in a bad place. We'll talk about it when I get home. We can start afresh. I'm thinking of university as well. That is after I retake my SAT's this year maybe. We have so much to catch up with.

Say hi to Juniper if you see her! If it wasn't for her I'd be long gone. I can't wait to get back and see her again. You and mum the most, I miss you and mum. That reminds me, is mum still worrying over every little thing? Tell her to take a chill pill and that her favourite son is returning home. Okay, kidding. We're both her favourite sons.

See you soon, baby brother.

Your loving arsehole of a brother,

Jere.

P.S when I come back and I see my stack of cigs gone, I will kill you. So you better stock up on cigs before I come home.

Juniper closed the letter and put it back into the envelope. She looked at the wall ahead of her with a blank expression on her face. Her heart throbbed and she closed her eyes trying to will away the tears that threatened to spill over. Jeremy Cox: the boy that Juniper Stauff saved.

Her mind and body were in two different places.

30th of August was a few days away. She could see Jeremy again. But if she was being entirely honest with herself she feared the day to come. They barely knew each other, a three year gap between their ages but Juniper had played a vital part in Jeremy's life. Except she hadn't wanted to. The thought of him wanting to meet her made her feel nostalgic.

She'd kept Dimitri waiting too long and she turned around with the intention of leaving. She could worry about this letter later.

The unexpected happened.

There laid Charlie Cox in bed. He was looking up at Juniper with both shock and angry. "What the fuck are you doing in my room at like one am in the bloody morning, June?!" fumed Charlie.

"Oh shit. Not again," Juniper Stauff said as Charlie's blazing stare burned holes into her head.

CHAPTER 9

Charlie Cox's eyes scanned the room before his eyes settled on his bed. He picked up the teddy bear and stared right into Juniper Stauff's eyes trying to figure out why she was in his room in the dead of the night, why he was cuddling with a teddy bear and why on earth he had shaving cream on his face. He knew that whatever the reason was, it wasn't pleasing at all.

"Uh," Juniper stuttered. "Well, good seeing you!" And she ran to the window, climbed through it and rushed to Dimitri's car running as if her life depended on it. The shouts from Charlie grew distant as her legs carried her away from that room, away from that letter and away from the unbearable memories.

Juniper slammed the door of Dimitri's run-down car and almost shouted, "drive!"

The further they travelled away from the Cox's household, the steadier her heartbeat became. Slowly but surely her heart beat returned back to normality.

Images of the past flickered across her mind and she shut her eyes in an instant, her hands fisting instinctively. Blood. All she could see was blood upon her hands. All she could hear were the screams that emanated from his throat. All she could smell was the alcohol from the tortured body beneath her hands. All she could do, all she was able to do, was black out.

No, she thought. She must not cry in front of Dimitri.

Dimitri sensed that something had gone wrong and he nudged Juniper to get her attention. "June, are you okay?"

"Huh?" she asked, dazed. Dimitri's voice had reeled her back to reality.

"Are you alright?" he repeated. He was sure that she was going to lie to him but he was wrong. Juniper had been doing a lot of that lately; lying. And he saw through the false pretense. He just wasn't sure if her intentions were pure and right, and more importantly, what they meant.

"I'm cool as a cucumber," she said, her lips curling up into a convincing smile. When Dimitri did not return the gesture she turned away and faced the window so he wouldn't be able to see the tears that were threatening to break through. "No," she said at last. "I feel terrible."

It was very hard to believe that Juniper could feel 'terrible'. She had always been rainbows and sunshine. He was ashamed of himself that after all these years of the friendship he was unable to spot her flaws and her little white lies. He fell for her façade like everyone else did. He had put his attention on entirely different matters.

"Do you want to talk about it?" he asked.

She swallowed down the lump that formed in her throat and looked back at Dimitri as a forced smile made its way to her lips. "I'd rather not," she smiled. "But how about we go to Eiling Beach?

There's this place that's there that is not only a good scenery but also a place to think things over and make sense of the shit in your life. It's my sanctuary in other words. Plus, it's only a fifteen minute drive!"

Dimitri knew better than to urge the situation and ask her what was really bothering her. While he knew that she wasn't on good terms with him for seeking revenge on Charlie, he knew that what put her into this stress was none of his doing. "Okay," he finally said and set his eyes on the road and they made their way to Eiling Beach.

The ride was full of silence and tension and while one would think that fifteen minutes was a matter of a short time, in this situation it stretched long and Dimitri felt like a million years passed before he parked his car in the parking lot. He felt sorry for Juniper. It was only her, other than his ex-girlfriend, whom he let himself get attached to. And even though they were close he pushed her away, afraid to share his demons with anyone who wasn't Amanda Obereen. Maybe it was infatuation what he and Amanda had. But he was certain that what he felt was not infatuation but love.

They got out of the car before Dimitri rounded his car so he could come face-to-face with Juniper. "So," he said, a bit awkwardly, "where is this special place?

A quirky smile graced her lips and she held out her hand. Chucking, Dimitri shook his head in mild amusement before he took Juniper's hand. She led him further into the beach, away from the noise of the campers and Dimitri became confused. Where was she taking him?

"Are you planning to take me away from here and to a dark alley so that you can murder me?" Dimitri joked, bemusement dancing in his eyes.

"Yes, because there are dark alley's in beaches and killing an individual would be a very Juniper-like thing to do," she said, her reply heavy with the weight of sarcasm. Juniper came to a halt and Dimitri almost bumped into her.

Catching his balance, he said, "have we arrived at the slaughterhouse yet? Doesn't look like a slaughterhouse to me." His eyes landed on the massive rock - actually it was rocks on top of rocks. The shadow they formed just looked like one big, gigantic rock. A humongous boulder would be a more fitting description.

Juniper rolled her eyes at him. "Follow me," she instructed as she let go of his hand. She climbed the rocks, her hands firm on them as she ascended. It was quite high. "Um, do we have to climb?" Dimitri asked, anxiousness lacing his voice.

"Wouldn't be any other way to get to the other side, Dimmy," Juniper said. "I thought you'd got ridden of your fright of heights. Or was that a lie to get me to stop bugging you?"

Dimitri could picture that confident smirk on her lips. Oh no, he thought confidently. He was not going to give her the satisfaction of winning. "I am not afraid of heights," he said defensively.

"Really?" she panted halfway up. "Prove it then, Dimmy."

Challenge accepted. He began to climb, trying to imitate her actions the further he went up but he clearly lacked in the hiking field - or any sport, really. By the time he was a quarter way up only a minute had passed but Dimitri felt like a year had just passed. The rocks had a fair amount of space between them so it wasn't all that hard to get a good grip and climb with one's own bare hands and feet. Unfortunately, for inexperienced people like Dimitri, it was a challenge that was proving hard to complete.

The climb down was easier than the climb up. There was less weight of the body to support as Dimitri climbed down compared to when he climbed up. After Dimitri descended on the other side, he looked at his surroundings.

A couple of metres from where he stood was a fence that was torn apart. The crack in the fence was enough space to let a body - the size of Juniper's - pass through.

After all, it was Juniper who created the hole in the fence. She wouldn't let such a materialistic thing keep her away from her sanctuary. She had passed through the hole and stood a few metres away from the fence waiting for Dimitri.

While she waited for him she closed her eyes and breathed in the beautiful fragrance of the silent night air. It was a wonder why the air was never stale or polluted. She was sure that the only reason the area was fenced was due to industrialization. But she could be wrong.

A lazy smile found its way to her lips as she let out a content sigh. There was just something about this exotic atmosphere that put her at ease and made her forget about her troubles and worries. She almost even forgot she brought Dimitri along.

"Whoa," she heard him say from behind her, his voice full of awe. She looked up at him and chuckled when she saw the awestruck expression on his face.

"I know," she replied as she returned her gaze back to the scenery. Right ahead of them laid lilies that floated upon the waving water with lily pads beneath them. The lilies floated back and forth, all in a synchronised motion and it was breath taking. They were standing on the rocks and they stared at the scenery that laid underneath their feet. It was beautiful and a brilliant view. Words failed to describe its extravagance.

They fell into a moment of blissful silence before she looked at him and smiled sadly. "I'm sorry," she said, a lump forming in her throat.

Dimitri was taken aback from her words. She had no reason to say those words so why had she said them? He faced her, tearing his gaze away from the lilies and his brows furrowed, confusion clear in his expression. "I am hundred percent sure that I have earwax in my ears. Did Juniper Stauff just apologize?"

Juniper tried to smile. She was usually the one who brought humour into their conversations but it seemed like the roles were reversed. And her attempt to smile went to vain. "Yeah, she did."

Dimitri cut the act and put on a serious expression. He turned his body so that she was directly in front of him. He wanted to see her face, to see if he could read between the lines of her non-joking expression. Only a few centimetres invaded their space but that didn't bother Dimitri. It was Juniper's recent attitude that seemed to bother him.

"I was wrong. I thought I was doing the right thing. But..."

This only confused him more. "Wrong? The right thing?"

She looked into his eyes and for the first time in forever she let her guard down. She let him read the emotion and the years worth of secrets she was so desperately intent on hiding. But secrets needed words to make another individual understand it. And in this situation Juniper was hopeful to hold onto it a little longer.

"I was wrong about you. About you and Amanda. About Charlie."

"June, what are you talking about?"

She looked up into his brown eyes. They somehow didn't feel like home anymore. She was seeking comfort but when she looked into those soft, brown eyes that she could once stare into all day long, she didn't feel so lost in them. She felt a little comfortable. He was her best friend after all. But there was this foreign feeling - a feeling she couldn't place her finger on.

"You all have somebody to lean on," she whispered, her voice cracking slightly. "You all have somebody to hold onto. You all have somebody in your lives that you know you can fall back on, help you get to your feet and take that ticket for the one hell of the journey you're going to take on. You know there's somebody that will be by your side, that will defend you and tell you right from wrong. You have that somebody in your life." Juniper's voice trembled and she faltered for a second. She looked at Dimitri in a manner that almost made her lose her power to speak. The way Dimitri was looking at her gave her heart a tight squeeze. On his face was a look of confusion coupled with sorrow and pity. "You have Amanda and likewise she has you. Charlie has his family, Jeremy."

Dimitri gave a somewhat tired sigh. "Amanda and I are over, June," he said, stressing on the word over. "And is Jeremy the name of Charlie's brother? I didn't know his name."

She decided not to say anything about Jeremy because his name itself hit home. "Amanda and you are over," she stated. "Not entirely, am I right? I know that there's still something, there's still chemistry, that she just didn't up and leave. She's that someone, Dimmy. And it won't be too long for her to realise that you're her someone too."

Juniper Stauff pressed her lips together and finally she let a tear spill over. Keeping back the tears was too much work and a waste of energy. Before she could wipe away the tear, Dimitri's hand flew up to her face and cupped her cheek. He slid his rough thumb over her cheek, brushing away the stray tear.

He understood what upset her. He knew what was coming. He didn't need words to know what was racing through her mind. But Juniper did. She hugged him, feeling his arms come around her torso after she threaded her arms around his waist. She loved the feeling of his arms around her, the fire that danced between their exposed skins.

"She's that someone, Dimmy," Juniper said at last. "She replaced me."

Dimitri held her at an arm's length as he pushed her back so he could get a proper view of her face. His hand brushed away the red-brown hair that covered her striking blue eyes from view. His hands cupped her face, his own face filled with sincerity.

"No one has replaced you," he said softly - reassuringly. His voice was barely above a whisper and that made Juniper's eyelids feel heavy making them droop just a little as his minty, fresh breath waved over her face. "No one can replace my Juniper Stauff." He paused and offered her a smile. "You have someone, June."

"No, I don't," she objected as she tried to look away and hide her embarrassment. But Dimitri Remirez wouldn't allow his best friend to hide. He made her look at him, his hands still firm on her face. He made her look into his eyes.

"You have me."

His words ignited a flame within her, lit up spark and her entire being lightened up. Those three words was all it took for Juniper to stand on her tiptoes and press her lips to Dimitri's, pouring all the years of secret love into that one affectionate kiss.

She pulled back, her eyes sparkling with excitement and her heart beating enthusiastically fast. But Dimitri stilled, his mouth wide open and shock swarm clear in his eyes. It was his reaction that made Juniper to back away, her excitement dying out instantly along with that glorious smile of hers.

She thought she would give it a try. She thought the proximity between them meant something to him. She thought she read the signs right. She was wrong.

"June," he whispered. She knew he didn't know how to let her down easy.

"Don't," she said, her voice wavered as she took a step back out of his embrace, the arms that once secured her fell away.

"I didn't mean it like that," Dimitri said in an attempt to defend himself.

She opened her mouth to tell him that she knew what his reaction to the kiss meant when a booming voice broke through the silent, breezy night. "You two!" came the sudden deep voice. Both Juniper's and Dimitri's head snapped towards the source of voice and their eyes met a fat policeman, his stomach bulging over his trousers. His stride was brisk and strict, his flabby arms moving up and down as he made his way to the two teenagers.

Once he got to them, the dark skinned man had a look of anger on his face. "There is a reason this area is fenced!" he said, his booming voice growing louder. "What are you two lovebirds doing out here?" Clearly, Mr Policeman didn't know that now was not the moment to interrupt them but Juniper was happy that he did. She couldn't face Dimitri. Her cheeks were burning, hot with embarrassment.

"I...we..." Dimitri started but fell short not quite sure what they were doing in a restricted area in the first place. His panicked gaze flew to Juniper, his eyes seeking for help. But she was too stunned by the turn of events and her raging emotions to even respond.

The policeman rolled his eyes and instructed Dimitri and Juniper to give him their backs as he cuffed them and took them to the police station where their parents would be called and informed of their children's trespassing activity.

Juniper turned back, the tears spilling down her cheeks as she let the cold metal of the cuffs scrape against her bare skin.

He didn't love her. Of course he didn't. But for a moment she had let her guard down and let hope plant its seed there in her body and grow. Juniper, in this awkward situation, finally knew what it was like to be in Dimitri's shoes; heartbroken.

CHAPTER 10

Juniper Stauff and Dimitri Remirez sat side by side in a cell as they both waited for their parents to bail them out. To say that they had both landed themselves into an awkward situation would be an understatement.

It was Dimitri who initiated the conversation. "I'm sorry," he said, turning to face her.

She smiled at him but he could tell it was forced. "For what, Dimmy?"

"Oh, cut the crap, June," Dimitri said. "Look, I didn't mean to hurt you. You know I could never hurt you." There was a tone of desperation in his voice.

"I know. You got pretty pissed when Eric Sanders tried to...rape me."

His eyes widened and they glossed with astonishment. "You remember?"

"Of course I do, Dimmy. Bits and pieces have come back to me but I was really drunk so I don't recall everything and I'm really glad that I don't recall much of that night because the snippets itself that have come back to me are pretty vivid and...haunting. And I know that you wouldn't hurt me because you were pissed as fuck when Eric Sanders hurt me. If you were that pissed that you beat him to the pulp - that's how he looked when he came to school - I can't fathom you hurting me."

Dimitri's eyes softened and he reached out for her hand, giving it a tight squeeze. The way she spoke, the terror clear in her eyes strung at his heart. He knew she was trying to reassure him but she looked awfully scared and that made his heart ache. He might not have feelings for her but that doesn't mean he didn't care for her. She was one of the people he cared for and Dimitri cared for such little people. "He was doing it without your consent and," he faltered not quite sure what to say next. "I've never seen you vulnerable, June."

Juniper's eyes were watering at this point and she tried to take a hold of reality. The façade she had built up, the amount of strength it took to build those walls around her - all of it was slipping away and Dimitri was finally going to get a look at exactly who his best friend was.

"Yeah," she said. "You cared for me, Dimmy. And I think that was the trap. I thought that maybe you had an inkling of feelings for me. I mean, yes, I know that you are in love with Amanda and Amanda is in love with you. That much was obvious. Even a blind man could see it. But I thought you felt something. Something, Dimitri. It probably wouldn't compare to as what I feel for you but I thought that there was a small part of you that likes me."

"I do like you, Juniper. There's a huge part of me that likes you. In fact, I love you. But not in the sense that you think," he said sympathetically.

"Or in the sense that I want you to," Juniper said as a small smile took over her lips. All Dimitri could see was sadness upon her face.

"Oh, June," he whispered, his grip around her hand tightening.

"No," she said indignantly, pulling her hand out of his grasp. "Don't you dare pull the pity card on me. I'm not in the mood for it."

They both looked at each other. Blue and brown eyes. They weren't the solution for each other's problems. Juniper would never tell him about the deal she made with Charlie. Everyone thought she was selfless. But she wasn't. She was selfish and that night she had taken part in something horrible - she went against her word because she thought it was for the better judgement. But it wasn't. And it was all soon going to come crashing down on her.

"An hour ago," Juniper said, breaking the silence that had reappeared, "you said that nobody could replace your Juniper Stauff. That gave me a little hope and then you said that I had you. That's what made me so sure that there might be something between us. But might is a pretty indefinite word, isn't it?" Juniper smiled sadly, playing with her fingers.

"I'm really sorry that I don't feel the same. I wish I did. But I don't. You deserve someone who loves you-"

"If it's the talk, Dimmy, I am not ready," Juniper interjected before Dimitri could say furthermore.

He chuckled at her response and she felt something in her heart lift. The thin ice was finally broken.

He looked at her then and said, "remember that day when I told you that you had everything you ever wanted and you said I had no idea how wrong I was?"

It was the day Juniper suggested that Dimitri take his revenge on Amanda Obereen. She remembered that clear as day. "Yeah?" she nodded.

Dimitri looked at his best friend straight in the eye. "Tell me what you don't have, June?" He looked and sounded desperate. Determination was one of the many emotions that laced his voice as he spoke - as if he could fix things, he wanted to fix Juniper.

"You mean other than you?" Juniper barked. Her voice had an underlying sinister tone and that took Dimitri mildly by surprise. He was still not accustomed to the fact that hatred and evil existed in the blood that flowed through her veins. Juniper couldn't be vile. Or so he had thought.

"I wish I hadn't done that," she whispered mostly to herself but Dimitri picked up on her words.

"Hadn't done what?" Dimitri questioned, slightly more curious than he cared to admit.

Juniper lifted her gaze to his and there was a pregnant pause before she spoke. "Kissed you," she said, her lips trembling. "I wish I hadn't kissed you."

He sighed deeply. "And I wish that it could-"

"No," she said fiercely, "you don't understand!" Then she gave out a light sigh as she looked down at her shaking hands. She didn't want him to see the tears that had now built up in her eyes. "You don't understand, do you?" she said lowly. "I kissed you and that was my mistake. I mean, yeah, I really do like you. But now that I've kissed you things won't be the same between us. Everything would be awkward and I don't want that. You're one of the few people of the male specimen that actually gives a shit about me. You care for me and...yes, I have this crush on you but there's some stuff I've learnt about you, stuff that don't need words to explain them. You showed me that friendship matters. That hopelessness exists. You showed me that having secrets is a burden. That the flames of guilt engulf you and you're soon burning out. You don't want to bring anyone else for the hell ride - except Mandy. Maybe you two really belong to each other."

Dimitri's expression morphed into one of shock and guilt. "How-how did you-"

"I'm supposed to be your best friend, Dimmy. I know a lot about you than you permit me to know," she replied his unfinished question.

"Do you," he began, "have any secrets, June?"

A smile touched her lips. It didn't hold much brightness as it once did before. Maybe because Dimitri's vision of Juniper was finally clearly and he was finally seeing through the opaque facade that had recently turned transparent.

"Not really," Juniper said. "I have no secrets to share. Nobody has ever asked me if I was hiding something. Maybe it's because I have this fake smile plastered to my lips and my character to others is seen as open and not secretive. Truly, I'm not. If they asked what I was hiding I would tell them what I was hiding. But no one has asked me who I fancied or who I had a crush on. Nobody asked if I sought the truth about my biological parents. Nobody asked if I actually found my bio parents, met them and felt disappointed at how they made me feel-"

Juniper was crying now, the tears that slowly made their way down her face had turned to sobs as she hunched over, covering her tear-streaked face with her cold hands. Dimitri felt a pang of sympathy and shifted closer to his best friend as his arms made their way around her petite body and brought her body close to his chest, resting his head on top of hers as she soaked his shirt with salty tears. It wasn't too soon that Dimitri felt himself trembling too. His hold around her tightened like he was sure he could protect her. But he couldn't for he could not even offer protection for himself - his father was the proof of that. That didn't make him stop trying though.

"I remember you telling me when we were almost twelve that you wanted to meet your biological parents. You wanted to know who they were, which one of them you looked more like, and most importantly why they weren't the ones who raised you. You were going through some sort of anger phase, I remember. But a few weeks later when I asked, you said you didn't care anymore and that you were happy with your parents. You didn't tell me you met your bio parents."

Juniper shrugged, lifting her head up so she could meet Dimitri's eyes. "I was bummed and you didn't bring it up after that." There was a short pause before she continued speaking. "I lied. I did care. I still do. Before I turned twelve I always talked about how I wanted to meet my bio parents. You remember that. But my adoptive parents said it was a bad idea. They both said I would be disappointed at the outcome and they weren't exactly lying. They both knew how badly I wanted to meet my bio parents though. I knew that my adoptive parents had become my family, I don't call them mum and dad for no reason. But I just wanted to know my blood, where I came from and why they sent me away.

"So two days after my twelfth birthday I came downstairs in the evening when I heard the bell ring. Mum and dad got to the door first and they were two strangers on our porch. Those two strangers were my bio parents."

Juniper backed away from Dimitri, wiping the tears with the sleeve of her black top. "My bio father was with another woman, many women in fact. My bio mother worked in a bar and did a part time job being a stripper. I was conceived in a shabby motel. My bio dad visited the bar so many times just to see my bio mother do her thing with the pole. When she told him that she was pregnant he left. He took off and the only time he ever saw her again was when Mum and Dad arranged a meeting with me. The stripper who was my biological mother bore me for nine months. I didn't like who my bio father turned out to be but I wasn't all that disappointed with my bio mother. She stayed longer than he did and told me that she would have kept me but she gave me away because she wanted me to have a clean life, a life she couldn't have. A life without chaos and drugs. Well, half of that came true. I'm kind of in the midst of chaos right now."

She let out a hollow laugh and it highly lacked humour. "So yeah, I dug myself into a hole my twelve year old self got out of. Mum and Dad are going to kill me when we're out."

"Your parents are less harsher to deal with," Dimitri said so low that if Juniper wasn't listening she would have missed it.

"Your dad?" she asked bringing up the topic she was very hesitant to face Dimitri with.

Dimitri's head shifted to her in an instant and he looked at her with a mixture of shock and awe. "How did you know?"

"I didn't really. But it wasn't so hard to guess. That night I sneaked out to see you, you were battered and bruised. The only conclusion I could come up with was that your father was the only one who could have done that to you since you two were the only ones having dinner." Her heart clenched at the mere thought of him getting hurt.

"Did you ever know why Mr Cox shot himself?" Dimitri asked, "why he committed suicide?"

Juniper shook her head. She never knew the reason and she never bothered to find out. Just as everyone in Sereneigo she assumed he suffered from depression. She deemed it immoral to snoop around in the business that was not hers.

"He had an affair with my Mum."

An involuntary gasp left Junipers lips as she stared with horror in her eyes at the boy beside her. "But..."

"We all know how much Charlie's parents loved each other. Charlie and his brother were very proud of their parents. Charlie would always talk about them. But, I guess, Mr Cox couldn't face his wife with his ever-growing guilt of cheating on her. And he was so overwhelmed with guilt that he ended up shooting himself in the head. Charlie's dad worked in the police force and Mrs Cox asked to cover up his suicide. But that didn't last for long because the whole of Sereneigo knows that Mr Cox was a coward. There are so many other rumours but what I said now is the plain truth because who else would know the truth? After all, it was my mother he cheated with."

"Oh my," Juniper said as she brought her hand up to her mouth.

"Mum told Dad about her affair. She didn't love Dad anymore or not as much as she once did. I was exposed to all of this news when I was almost ten. I was so young and Mum or Dad surely didn't bother to sugar-coat the truth before telling me this shit. When Mum took off with some stranger Dad fell into depression. He used to - and still does - drink away his sorrows. He blames himself for not being a good husband. He blames me for not being the son they - he - wanted. Each day I lost a small piece of my Dad until one day he lashed out. He took out all his anger and frustration on me. And like the good boy I've always been I stood my ground and took the beating."

Juniper watched as Dimitri's hands shook with fear and sorrow. Tears had surfaced to his eyes. "Dimmy," Juniper whispered, "you can't do this to yourself. Look at me!" And when he looked at her she said, "you have to do something. You can't let him do that to you. Report him or-"

"No!" he exclaimed. "He's my dad, June. I still love him despite the horrid things he's done to me. I know that deep down my father is still there. He hasn't been himself these past years but I'm sure I can bring him back. I'm his son. I can bring him back. I can," Dimitri cried, "I can bring him back. I can..."

Juniper comforted Dimitri as she let him bring his head to her shoulder and weep. "I can bring him back," he whispered, choking on his own sobs. "I can bring him back," he repeated once more, hugging his best friend and caving into the warmth and care that her embrace provided.

He was lying to himself. Dimitri couldn't bring back his father. Nobody could.

CHAPTER 11

J uniper Stauff and Dimitri Remirez spent the next two days at home, both of them still living in the events that occurred the previous night.

Juniper begged her parents to stay home and they reluctantly agreed on the condition that she was to prepare them lunch on the weekends as well as the two days she took off. It wasn't much of a fuss considering Juniper loved to cook. Well, she loved to bake but how different could cooking be from baking? This was her time to go all out and impress her parents - a way of saying sorry and earning extra cookie points.

She was grounded till God knows when. Her parents hadn't really made up their mind. She suggested graduation but they thought six months was too short of a time. She knew they would cool down eventually but for the moment being, they were furious.

"What in Heaven's name were you thinking?" her mother burst, her dark face glowering in anger when they arrived home from the police station.

"We know how much you care for that boy but June," her father exclaimed, "you were out there alone in the night. God knows what he could have done to you."

"Dad, he's Dimitri! He wouldn't do anything to me," she replied defensively even though a small part of her was angry at the rejection that Dimitri gave her.

"I know, honey, but what the hell were you thinking? You can't just trespass areas. It was a fenced off area for a reason, Juniper!"

"You two don't get it," she cried. "That place is like my second home-"

"Well, you should have let it go when that area was fenced! I don't know what construction is going on there but that is now private property and you have no right to venture into zones like that. Who knows what they are doing there or what hazards lay there? You could have gotten hurt."

"Look at me. I'm alive."

"Are you trying to be sarcastic, Juniper Anna Stauff?" her mother scolded, her dark face glowering even more. "Don't you dare talk back to your father in that manner!"

"Get it into that fanatical brain of yours. June, stop living in the fantasy world and start living in the real world."

Juniper was recalling this conversation that had happened as she sat on her bed, her mind still reeling with the recent events that led up to her present. She never let her father's words hurt her. She knew better than to take an angry man's word to heart when he was merely trying to protect his only child. She knew her parents better than anyone. While they never gave out harsh judgements, they gave out extreme punishments to ensure that history would not repeat itself. They were simply scared out of their wits to what could have happened to their daughter.

She reached over the bed and grabbed her phone before lying back down on her pillow. She stared at her cell for a while as she contemplated calling Dimitri. Should she call him? Would he even pick up? Dimitri was well known to have his phone on him for the most part of his life. Giving in, she pressed the third number on her speed dial.

Dimitri picked up on the sixth ring. "Hello?" he greeted, his voice groggy.

"Oh, were you sleeping?" "June!" he exclaimed and she heard a few noises in the background mixed with a few strangled groans. "Hey, I wasn't expecting you to call."

"You didn't go to school either?" she asked, playing with the ends of her hair, twirling them within her finger. She was hesitant to call Dimitri. Would everything return back to normal after everything that happened? She feared It wouldn't but in that moment it was the most that she wanted.

"No, I'm really sore. My dad left town after he came to pick me up from the police station. He won't be back for two days."

There was silence on Juniper's side of the line. What was she supposed to say? After the short crackling silence, she took a deep breath and came up with a question. "Does he often do that? Just up and leave, I mean?"

The tension was clear even through the phone. "Yeah, when things get really bad."

"What do you mean when things get really bad?"

Dimitri hesitated. "He has bad people for company," was all Juniper got for an answer and while she wanted more, maybe a better detailed answer, she knew now was definitely not the time to pressure him to tell her anything. Especially when she wanted him to do something that she was sure he was going to decline.

She played with the card in her hand, turning it over several of times. Then a light bulb went off in her head. "I've got an amazing idea!" she blurted, not aware that she was still holding the phone to her ear and mouth.

"Oh no," Dimitri groaned from the other side of the line. "No more of your amazing ideas."

Juniper quickly covered her tracks up, glad that her small pause didn't hint anything to Dimitri. "Well, at least you admit my ideas are amazing," she teased.

"And stupid," he added.

"Whatever," she said as she rolled her eyes to herself. "Anyway, I've got a few hours to kill and my parents won't be home because it's date night today and I thought maybe I could swing by your house and we could watch a funny movie, or a Disney movie-"

"That's a horrible idea," Dimitri interjected.

"Welcome back, Grumpy Dimitri," Juniper retorted jokingly as she tried to hide the hurt from seeping into her voice.

She heard a chuckle from the other end of the line and her lips lifted up on their own accord and formed a pretty smile on those plush, pink lips of hers.

"Grumpy Dimitri doesn't exist," he said, his voice serious but his voice held large volumes of humour. She knew he was smiling too. "And neither does Great Juniper."

Juniper gasped, feigning hurt. "How dare you? I'm very great, thank you very much," she said, her voice teasingly curt.

He laughed before the humour in his voice died down and he returned back to serious. Juniper could almost picture the exhausted look on his face. "Look, June, I didn't mean to sound rude when I said that it's a horrible idea for you to come over. I just - I'm in a bad state right now. I look really revolting and I'm not going bother sugar coating the truth. I really got it from my dad last night. I just need rest, okay?"

But Juniper Stauff had always been stubborn. She could hear the brokenness of his voice. "Why do best friends exist?" she asked. "I'm always here to help. See you in fifteen." And before he had the chance to object or argue, she hung up.

Juniper put the ladder she found in the garden shed against the wall of Dimitri's house. There was no way Juniper could enter through the front door since she knew it was locked and the way Dimitri spoke was like he was in a hell load of pain. She wondered if he could even get off his bed to get to his bathroom. So she chose to go in through the way she did it the last time.

She gripped the cold metal of the ladder and ascended it. Once she reached the window, which was she was glad was open, she shifted her weight onto the sill and clambered into the room, tripping over her own foot and landing face first onto the floor with a loud thud.

She felt the pain of the fall move from head to toe and she held in the shudder of pain as she forced herself to get up. "Ow," she groaned. She couldn't help it as she felt the pain move all over her face and limbs.

"That was a dramatic entrance," Dimitri commented before he chuckled.

"Ha-ha," she replied, rolling her eyes. "Very funny."

"Oh, wow. That's a drastic change from Grumpy Dimitri to Funny Dimitri," he teased. He couldn't deny that he felt good that the kiss that transpired - well, transpired wouldn't be the appropriate word since he didn't kiss her back and the kiss was totally one sided - between them didn't affect their friendship.

Juniper lifted her gaze up to him after she dusted herself off the floor. Her mouth was turned into a scowl and ready to throw a comeback at him. But once her eyes settled on Dimitri she was rendered speechless.

Dimitri laid on his bed. He was shirtless and the only piece of clothing he was wearing was his boxers.It wasn't the half nudity that made her retort her stuck in her throat. It was his chest and the new slashes across them. New scars were bound to be formed, the slashes of the wounds still looked fresh and horribly pink and they were bound to layer over the old scars that didn't look as bad but still succeeded in making the lump in Juniper's throat to grow bigger.

His face was worse. While it was untouched, the scar that he received from his father never grew less prominent and it seemed far away from fading. It was the expression that he wore that seemed to rip Juniper's heart in two. It was terror-stricken, hurt and tired. He looked so damaged that Juniper had to do her level best not to cry when she opened her mouth.

"Dimmy," she said at last, her surprised and somewhat frightened eyes travelled around his torso, her eyes wandering from one fresh slash to the next. She willed her legs to carry her to Dimitri's bed and as she walked towards him, almost shakingly, she barely felt the tiles of the floor beneath her. Her brain was numb and still in shock as she laid herself down, perching herself on the edge of the bed and gingerly lifting a hand to his face.

"I told you it bad a horrible idea to come over," he said, his lips tilting up into a smile but Juniper didn't buy the fake cheeriness. It was a sorrowful smile. The worst kind of sad smiles. It hurt Juniper.

"Oh, Dimmy," she whispered, tears outlining her soft blue eyes. Hold back the sobs, she told herself but it was harder said than done, especially when one of the people you cared about the most almost looked like they were going to die. "Why did you let him do this to you?"

Dimitri's heart hammered within his chest but slowly as he welcomed Juniper's touch, his heart rate slowed. He lifted his hand and laid it on top of her hand that cupped his cheek, hiding his ugly long scar from view. "I can't stop him."

"Yes, you can and you know it-"

"June!" he cut her off with an edge to his voice that finalised this conversation. She wasn't going to get another word in this conversation and she knew that. She sighed then, letting out a puff of air as she blinked rapidly in an attempt to get rid of her tears.

She looked away, closing her eyes and trying to distract herself from the boy in the bed. But Dimitri didn't give herself long enough to collect her thoughts, feeling and composure. He said, "you told me everything you've hidden and kept secret, in the prison cell, right?"

When she looked back at him, her brows furrowed but inside she was panicking. What did he know? Her first thought flew to Charlie and the plan. "Yes, of course," she replied, the lie slipping off her tongue effortlessly.

"Why are lying to me, June?"

Her breath caught in her throat. Time froze. "I'm not lying," she said, trying to keep her heart in check.

"You are."

"Yeah?" she questioned, raising an inquisitive brow. "What gives you that ridiculous idea?"

"The letter," he replied firmly. Her heart skipped a beat. Did she see the letter Jeremy wrote to Charlie? But that was impossible because he was in the car the whole time and how could he have connected the dots so easily and fast? But then Dimitri explained and her heart began to race in panic but now for a whole new different reason.

"We went to your house to study and you just bolted to the bathroom because you had a desperate urge to pee," Dimitri explained, "and you told me to grab anything from the fridge in the kitchen. After I took out a Pepsi can, I saw a letter on your kitchen counter. And yes, I had no right to look at it or meddle in your affairs without your permission but you were taking awfully long in the bathroom and the letter just kept staring at me. Plus, it was already open so you wouldn't have noticed if I read it. I gave into curiosity and that's how I found out."

Juniper stared at him, shocked and angry. "You had no right to read that letter," she said, almost shouting.

"I know, but–"

"How dare you butt into my personal life–"

"You wanted to know everything about me when you hid the fact that you have–"

"Shut up!" Juniper screamed, pulling her hair in frustration. She got up from the bed, taking several steps away from Dimitri and she stared at him with a hateful look in her eyes. "I guess now you know why I kissed you. Life's too short and I couldn't risk having the opportunity throwback at my face-"

"Well, it did! It's not like I kissed you back, is it?"

His words sliced through her and the pool of tears that had gathered in her eyes, spilt over and came rolling down her cheeks in an ugly manner. She looked torn and hurt.

His eyes softened instantly. "June, I-"

"No," she said firmly. "No, you're right. You're always fucking right, Dimmy. But there's one thing you're wrong about and that's your father. Why can't you see that he's hurting you and that you have a choice. You can end this torture, Dimitri."

His eyes were guarded. He winced as he tried to push himself upright on the bed. "I can't do that to him," he whispered.

Their fights had never lasted for long. Juniper rushed forward and took her place back on the edge of the bed beside Dimitri. "You're not doing anything cruel to him," she whispered back. She was only recently exposed to physical abuse that Dimitri was getting by his father but already she couldn't handle it. She was so close to taking matters into her own hands.

"Reporting him to the police is not cruel?"

It isn't when you think about all that he's done to you, she thought quite bitterly. Instead, she pulled out the card she was playing with earlier when she was on the phone with Dimitri and handed it over to him. "Putting him in rehab to get over his alcoholic addiction is a better choice."

Dimitri's eyes scanned the words and while she wasn't touching him she could practically feel it from the air how tense his body got all of a sudden. When he looked up to her, he said, "get out."

Juniper was stunned. "What?"

"You heard me," he said, more angrily and loudly, "get the fuck out of my house."

Juniper stared at him. "Dimmy," she tried to reason.

But before she could actually get any words out, he said, "I told you that I can take this. That I can't stand up to my father. Putting him in this mental place won't do him good-"

"It'll do him plenty good!" Juniper shouted, slightly surprised by her own bravery. "And this 'mental place' helps people, for your information," she said vigorously as she used air quotations making Dimitri look ridiculous.

"Go away, June, and just leave me for a while to think. I'll see you in school, day after tomorrow-"

"Dimitri-"

"Get out, Juniper!" He screamed this time, his eyes holding a look of anger that Juniper had not seen before in her long thirteen years of friendship with him. An anger blazed in her eyes. How could he be so naive.

So she stomped to the end of his room, gripped the ladder and descended in as fast as she could. The anger was burning alive in her system and she jogged away from the house until she was far away enough to make a phone call. Acting on impulse, with the wild anger only blossoming in her system, she pulled out her phone from her back pocket and dialled the police emergency number. When the receptionist picked up, she poured all the information about Dimitri and his father into the phone along with her untameable anger.

She just wanted to help. There was nothing wrong in that intention of hers, was there?

CHAPTER 12

The second Juniper Stauff set foot on Phantom High grounds, whispers filled her ears. She parked her car in a rush, got out and headed towards the school doors to look for Dimitri. He wasn't answering her texts or calls and Juniper didn't think it was right of her to visit him when he clearly wasn't in the mood for his daily Juniper dose. Let's face it, she's one of the few people that can crack a smile to those lips of his.

The whispers that littered the atmosphere in the hallway and corridors were much worse than in the parking lot. Juniper tried not to feel affected by it all but how could she not when she was the one that caused this in the first place?

"Charlie is gay?"

"Oh Lord, is that shaving cream on his face?"

"He sleeps with a teddy bear. Well, screw trying to get into his pants."

"Who do you think did it?"

"I heard Charlie was looking for Juniper."

"June? Maybe it was Dimitri since Amanda did hook up with Charlie."

Juniper was nearing her locker, the whispers on this part of the corridor much less than through the entrance. A sullen looking Charlie Cox stood there slumped against her locker and she felt a sudden lump rise to her throat. What was he going to do to her?

"Charlie," she said, the slight emotion of fright seeped into her speech.

His head shot up from staring at his shoes and when his gaze met hers, his soft features turned hard and stony as a fire blazed within his eyes. He grabbed Juniper's hand and yanked on her wrist, dragging her down the corridor. No one bothered to look at them. They all seemed to be heading in another direction. What was all the commotion on the other side about? Juniper wondered.

"Charlie, listen, I can explain-" she was cut off as he opened the Janitor's closet and shoved her into the room, banging the door harshly behind him. His whole demeanour shook with anger. He was furious.

"What the fuck is wrong with you?" Charlie roared.

Juniper bit her lip as she tried not to cower at the proximity and his towering figure. "I...I didn't mean to-" she said, struggling to get the words out.

He backed away, sighing as a look of disbelief took over his angry features. He leaned on the wall and ran a hand through his messy, blonde hair. "When you saved my brother I was more than just happy. I could have been the most happiest, most excited person to exist that day. I could have never hated you, June. You are pretty, smart as hell and you're damn nice. You gave me absolutely no reason to hate you. When you saved my brother you gave me more reason to like you. You were a great friend and I honestly don't know what I did to you to make you stab me in the back like this. Now...now I am certain that I hate you."

His glare burned holes through her and she felt her heart twist. She wanted to shout out, "I didn't do anything!" But that would be a lie since she was the one who initiated this whole revenge plan.

"I told you I owed you a favour," he said. "You just saved my older brother. I meant what I said that day at the hospital. You were my brother's saviour so I owed you big time. I said I'll do any favour you wanted even if it was awfully harsh but I wasn't thinking then. I was just a ball of emotions that day. And I never thought you'd ask me a favour so harsh anyway so no harm was done. Or so I thought."

His glare grew more intimidating the more he talked of the history that transpired between them. "There's always a price to pay, isn't there?" he said, after running an exhausted hand over his face. "Yes, at first Amanda was dared to play with Remirez's heart and that's why she accepted his offer after she declined him. But soon she fell for that boy and I have no idea what she see's in Remirez and as much as I hated him, I cared more for my friend's happiness. I don't know if you stereotype us, popular kids, June, but I didn't care which social status the dude was from to make Amanda happy. That's what friends do, right? They look out for each other and make sure they are happy? You certainly did the opposite of that."

The more Charlie spoke, the more Juniper felt hurt. She felt the knife drive into the arc of her back and turning in the pit of her stomach. "We are friends, Charlie-" she started.

"Friends?" he barked out, a maniac laugh escaping his lips. "Oh no, dearest June. Not anymore. See, when you came to me telling me that now would be a good time to do you that favour I promised to do, I was all in. I didn't actually think you had the capability of making this favour I had to do for you so cruel. You said something about having a crush on Remirez and trying to make him notice you. I told you that that wasn't going to happen since Amanda and him were clearly in love. Then you told me you had a plan."

He leaned off the door, his posture rigid. "I wasn't okay with the plan. But you saved my brother and that meant a hell lot to me. Plus, I've always been a man of my words. Unlike some people," he added as he shot a look at Juniper. But she merely stood there like a coward, swallowing down the lump in her throat only for it to rise back up. "I did as you told me and I told Amanda that the game was still on and if she didn't choose popularity over Dimitri then all her friends would turn against her. Mandy didn't believe me. Why would she when I was the one who encouraged her to date Dimitri when she truly had feelings for him and cut this whole prank we were supposed to play on him? I don't know what I said but I made it pretty convincing that she had to choose. Looks like you aren't the only great liar out in the world, June."

Everything that he said somehow directed at her and she couldn't blame him for what he was doing. After all she deserved this treatment but it still hurt. Charlie had never acted so vile to her and now that he was, she was a little frightened. She was more hurt than frightened.

"For a second she made me believe that she was going to choose Dimitri but she didn't. She chose popularity and that made me think over my initial thoughts of her love for Dimitri. If she really loved him then she would have stayed with him. But she didn't stay with him and that action itself convinced me that she wasn't really in love with him. But I'd catch her watching Dimitri from afar with a longing look in her eyes and that's when I realised that we're all liars. Not just you and me, June. Every fucking person is a liar. But you're the best of them, right?"

When she didn't reply to his accusing comments and glare, he continued with his rant. "Then you wanted me at some party. Brooke's, was it? You wanted me to make a scene with Amanda. You wanted to ditch Dimitri there so he would come after you like a lost puppy and you'd get him drunk and who knows what else you had planned in that genius brain of yours? You didn't bother telling me the whole plan. You only told me to kiss Mandy and make a scene and that you were going to ditch Dimitri so he would come after you like a lost puppy after he saw me with Mandy. I was angry but I said I'd do it and this was the end of our deal. I was no longer in debt and you wouldn't mess me up in this horrible plan of yours. I made you promise because I thought if one thing you were good at was keeping promises. But you broke it as well!"

Then he glared at her and Juniper witnessed the tears gather up in his eyes. She only ever saw Charlie frustrated once and that was three years ago when they were going through a rough patch with his brother, Jeremy Cox.

He took a step forward and she took a step backward. With every step that Charlie took forward, Juniper took an equal amount of steps backward. She had never felt so intimidated by his tallness before. He had on a mask of anger, his nostrils flaring as his cheeks were tinted pink and his eyes sparkling with intense hatred.

"You know what I am now because of you? I'm gay. I've got nothing against gay people. I've got friends that are gay and I have no problem with that. But here's a fact that you apparently didn't know: I'm not gay and the girl I've been pining after this past month can't even look at me the same way. I liked her and I was going to ask her out on a date. But you ruined that. She acts differently, like I'm not a special guy but one of her girlfriends. She used to talk to me all flirtingly but today morning she started talking to me about nail polishes and how she was so proud of me for coming out. You screwed up almost every chance I had with that girl. Fuck you, Juniper Stauff."

She felt her knees wobble and she felt the prickling tears behind her eyes threaten to break through but she had held herself together.

"My parents are catholic as well. This news gets to them and I'll be so fucked. Is your life mission to ruin everyone in order for you to get your happiness that was never really yours in the first place?" Then he took one last step forward and closed the distance by pushing her against the wall and blocking her from any escape routes. He pointed his index finger at chest, his hands trembling as he spoke. "Tell me, did your lover boy put you up to this?"

"N-no," she instantly defended, stuttering in the process. "I did it. I thought I c-could win Dimitri over that way."

Juniper had known better than to go along with Dimitri's crude plan. She knew it would not end well so why did she bother standing in the way? Oh yeah, that's right, she thought he was her key to happiness. Now she had just turned everything upside down. Way to go, June, she thoughts to herself.

Charlie backed away from her, his features changing. A look of disbelief captured his looks. "You did this to me? I mean, of course I thought it was you since you were the one in my room and I didn't catch a glimpse of the car you ran off in but I thought you were going to deny it. Wow, I actually gave you a second thought." His features softened slightly as the hurt in his expression grew more evident. "After the favour I just did for you, you do this to me? You know, everyone says that you're a nice, sweet girl who genuinely cares about everyone's well being. What you did - putting those pictures up of me with words gay written in huge, fancy letters was anything but nice and sweet. I guess your action proved everybody wrong but they don't know that. I think I finally understand why they always keep saying, 'do not judge a book by it's cover.' Thanks for making me understand it."

Charlie Cox had smirked then but it wasn't all that attractive. It was sinister and evil and Juniper hated that his smirk could send waves of fear down her spine. "I'm finally seeing you for who you are," he said. "And I'm glad we're not friends anymore. Thanks for caring about my life." Then with a flash of anger in his eyes, he lashed out, "you know what? You are Juniper Stauff. What else? You are a fucking fraud."

He spat at her, glowering down at her. Then he did the unexpected. Charlie Cox pressed Juniper Stauff against the wall, his body moulding against hers in a rough manner as he pressed his lips harshly against hers. Juniper was stunned and had not a clue of what to do. Charlie then took her hands and brought them up to his head and her fingers found them threading through his hair from his persisting will to get her to kiss him back.

Juniper didn't know how long she had stood there like a statue but she was sure that Charlie was kissing her for over thirty-two seconds. She had lost count after that. Why he was doing this, Juniper didn't know but she knew he was going to benefit from this heated and furious kiss. No matter how pleasurable the kiss felt - there was no denying that his lips did good work - she knew it was wrong. It felt wrong and it definitely didn't turn her on. He wouldn't just kiss her out of the blue without purpose.

Then he pulled back and distanced himself from Juniper. He ran his hand through his messed up hair and looked down at his shirt that stood in odd angles now. Looking back up at her, he smirked as if to say, 'mission accomplished'.

"That would do it," he said, his swollen, pink lips stretching into a bigger smirk. Juniper's faced paled at his words as she ran her eyes over his appearance. She knew exactly what he had done; to prove that he wasn't gay when he walked out of the janitor's closet like he spent seven minutes in heaven with Juniper coming out the door as well.

"People won't fully buy this," he said gesturing to his appearance, "but maybe Kristie will look at me the way she used to. And at least I'm trying to fix what you destroyed. Though that was your job but apparently now it's mine."

"Charlie-" she had begun but she couldn't say anymore for he thrust open the door and left. She walked out, trying to catch his attention but as soon as she was out the door, all eyes landed on her and her heart sunk.

"Did Charlie Cox and Juniper Stauff just hump in the Janitor's closet?" was one of the few whispered questions that reached her ears and her face became paler if that were possible.

She caught Amanda's eyes from within the crowd and her heart leapt to her throat when Amanda threw her a disgusted look before turning and walking away from the crowd. Oh God, Juniper thought. She knows.

She lost yet another friend that day.

The whispers along the corridors grew worse as some people debated if Charlie Cox was really gay or not. Most knew that Charlie had always fancied girls and wondered who was brave enough to pull this crude joke on Charlie. Juniper made her way to the notice board to see exactly how much damage both she and Dimitri caused.

There were several pictures that coated the board. Charlie was half naked in all of them, boxers was all the clothing he seemed to be sporting. In some pictures, he had shaving cream around his face, while in other pictures he was hugging the teddy bear to his chest. Then there was one large picture that stood in the centre of all the embarrassing pictures; Charlie had shaving cream all over his face, he was hugging the teddy bear with a content smile slung over his lips as he continued to suck at his thumb. On the very top of board held a banner saying The Popular Jock, Charlie Cox: Gay?

Oh no, she thought. She knew that most people didn't believe that Charlie was gay by just this little prank but nobody ever dared step up to Charlie. He wasn't exactly the stereotypical bad boy but he could pick a mean fight when he was furious. This was all her doing. Sure, it was Dimitri who did this but if she had never initiated the revenge plan then Dimitri wouldn't have thought of this.

Juniper rushed to the bathroom forgetting that her next class was due to start in a minute. She had already heard the warning bell go off yet she locked herself in a cubicle and started crying, the sobs that were held back for so long slipped out from her mouth in ugly wails.

Yes, Dimitri was hot, cute, nice, kind and her best friend. But his love belonged to someone else and that someone else was not Juniper. She just took so long to see it. This was her doing, this was her fault. It was her reckless thoughts that caused all this havoc and a rift between her most valued friendships. It was her fault.

It was all her fault.

CHAPTER 13

Juniper Stauff had her head in her hands as she listened to her parents drone on about the one subject she could never be able to make them shut up about it.

"June, baby, please be reasonable-"

"For the last time no!" she said, raising her voice by just a notch over her own mother's voice.

But Merliah Stauff had this conversation several with her daughter to be affected by her tone or words. She just wished that Juniper would see the seriousness of the situation and know that this wasn't something to joke around with. Juniper's life was certainly precious but whether Juniper saw that or not, she didn't know because she was declining the treatment that Merliah persisted on so much.

"Look, I'm late for school-" Juniper started.

"It doesn't matter," Juniper's father scolded, his dark face burning with anger and frustration. "This is more important than school."

Juniper was obviously in a foul mood. Her parents could tell by the comments she threw at them that she was in no mood to talk about this. But then again, she was never in the mood to talk about it. Juniper's eyes moved to the clock and she looked back at her parents with a sour expression. "Thanks mama," she said shooting a look at her mother who had done most of the talking the moment Juniper stepped into the kitchen. "I already missed first period."

Merliah's face softened and she gathered her daughter's hands in her own, giving them a tight encouraging squeeze. "Please, baby, you have to see that your parents want you around as long as they are around."

"I don't want treatment," Juniper said firmly that finalised the conversation and before her mother or father could get another word out of their talkative mouths, she shot up from the chair, grabbed her bag in a fast, snake like motion and ran out of the house. She was tired of this. It had been almost a month since the revelation, since the letter - the very letter that Dimitri apparently read. But look at her. She was doing fine. She didn't need treatment and if she did, well, she didn't want it. She hadn't yet reached any critical stage so no rash decisions needed to be taken.

When she parked her car in the school parking lot, she saw a familiar figure leaning against a car nearby. Juniper's heart jumped to her throat once she got out of the car and he spotted her. He had a murderous look in his eyes and when he started to advance towards her, she spun on her heel and headed the opposite direction. She knew by the infuriated look that took over his adorable features that things for her were not going to end well.

She had always been the sportier one but she didn't have Dimitri's long legs. He caught up to her pretty quickly and latched his hand onto her arm, spinning her around so that she could face him. She lifted her eyes, hesitant as a building sense of panic inflated within her chest. He looked slightly out of breath, a tinge of red tinted his cheeks lightly.

"I'm late for class," Juniper said as she tried to escape.

But his hold around her arm tightened and when looked her dead in the eye, she cowered as she gave out a light sigh and stopped fighting against his hold. Finally he let go of her, his eyes blazing with anger like she had never seen before. She had never seen Dimitri this angry.

"Why?" was the first thing that shot out of his mouth, his harsh words seemingly louder than the deafening silence.

She swallowed. "Why what?" she asked trying to act as naïve and innocent for as long as she could.

"Stop shitting with me, Juniper," he said, her full name rolling off his tongue in a violent manner. She always preferred it when people called her June, especially Dimitri because he had a slight British accent that made her name sound beautiful. He rarely called her Juniper and by the way he uttered her whole name she knew he was beyond angry. This was serious.

"I'm sorry," she began, taking a deep breath.

"Are you?"

"I am-"

"Doesn't seem like it."

A sudden anger washed over her. Who was he to tell her what to do and what not to do? Could he not see that he was suffering? How more blind could he get? "You're right," she lashed out as she crossed her arms across her chest and looked at Dimitri with fury. "I'm not sorry. I did the right thing and you know it."

"The right thing?" Dimitri laughed, his maniac laugh echoing around the parking lot. His laugh made Juniper's heart twist the slightest bit but she decided to keep on her straight face. She wasn't going to pity him and his humourless laugh. She was going to fight for what she thought was right.

"Are you a coward or a fighter, Dimitrius Josh Ramirez? Because you taking your father's shit, letting him do all those horrible things to you for eight continuous years is not an act of bravery. That is not what a fighter would do. You know what a fighter would do, Dimmy? He'd fight back. If you were a fighter, you would fight your father back. You would win this little war you and him got going on. Obviously you don't physically attack him but putting him in a rehabilitation centre where he could recover with professional help would have been the best solution-"

"But instead you chose to report him," Dimitri spat out, his face a hair's breadth away from hers, fury and hurt and many other conflicted emotions flickered across his eyes.

She backed away from him, the closeness of their bodies didn't help Juniper's metaphorical healing heart. It was making the process of healing harder. So she took a couple of steps backward but her new fiery side that had a tendency of popping up the at most unexpected times lately didn't wash away by his retort.

"Well, I was angry and if you ask me, he deserves what he got. I have no idea how Amanda put up with this crap and didn't do something. I know that she loves you and obviously she loves you more than I did because she can't risk losing you. Guess what, Dimmy? I've lost so much so I guess losing your friendship just adds to the list."

He was silent for a moment, his brown eyes had softened con-siderably at her small speech but Juniper could tell that he was still tense because he looked stiff and his jaw was still locked into place. Then he let out a tired sigh, his glare now less harsher than it was before. "You're a selfish bitch," he said.

His comment took Juniper completely by surprise. By his change in mood and the atmosphere that shrouded them, this was not the comment she expected him to make. However much his words made the hole in her heart widen up, she swallowed down than pain and hurt of the words and put on her brave face. The fake smile; the facade that everyone around her was so used to. "Tell me something I don't know," she said, tilting her head as a deviously innocent smile crept its way to her pink-glossed lips.

Her action and response reignited the anger within Dimitri and he stared at her, shocked, bewildered and infuriated. He took a step closer and she took a step back. They repeated this action a few times until Juniper's back hit the door of an unfamiliar car and she was left with no escape.

"Reporting my dad to the police was none of your business," he seethed through clenched teeth and Juniper felt his minty breath fan over her face. He still didn't look so good after she last saw him and she was glad that he was okay now and back on his feet. Up close, the scar that graced his face looked so terrifying and Juniper held in the urge to run her hand down the jagged line. Despite how glad she was that he was no longer being physically abused, she was still very, extremely, outrageously angry.

"And reading that letter on the counter was any part of your business?" she shot back, baring her teeth as she squinted her eyes and glared at him with as much hate and anger she could summon.

He stepped away from her, her words hurting him. The hurt that he experienced then was written well across his face, the hurt etched itself clearly into his features and Juniper could see that her words finally hit him. He had no right to read the letter, to even give into temptation of reading it. Of course, her feelings were a little hypocritical because Juniper was constantly giving into temptation for the past few days but she was angry and hurt just as he was and she, just like him, picked up anything to throw back into his face and defend herself.

"Remember when I said that you were incapable of being a bitch even if you tried? And you somehow felt that offensive? Well, I don't think you'll feel offended any longer. You are a bitch. A fucking, lying, backstabbing bitch. We're done."

Without a second glance or without giving Juniper the chance to speak up and provoke him by throwing further insults in his face, he whirled on his heel, gave his back to her and walked away from Juniper. Dimitri left her petite, broken self all alone in the parking lot.

Juniper Stauff had just lost her most precious friend and her mind was reeling with the sudden event to even comprehend this fact.

Juniper Stauff was anything but happy. The week had passed by slower than a snail's pace, the days stretching long and the nights filled with a deafening silence. Peace was restored back in Phantom High but this time it wasn't Juniper who had fixed the peace. She wasn't the hero she claimed to be and over the slow days that passed by, her mind reeled with the thoughts of recent events and she began to acknowledge her mistakes. Charlie was right; Juniper was not selfless but selfish. Dimitri was right; Juniper was a cold, mean bitch. Everyone who was exposed to her sudden actions and cruelty knew how to distinguish fake Juniper from sincere Juniper.

Even Amanda Obereen was ignoring her. Juniper was consumed with her hate for Amanda, all due to the fact that Amanda had the capability of stealing Dimitri's heart and she didn't, that she forgot why Amanda and her were friends. Juniper and Amanda's friendship started long before Dimitri and Amanda became a couple and it was a fact that Amanda and Juniper were the most weirdest, craziest and closest friends ever. Was Dimitri's love worth so much that she began to hate the person who was with her through most of life's traumas?

Dimitri and Amanda were back together. Dimitri must have told Amanda everything, he must have came clean since every time Amanda passed Juniper in the halls she'd look at her with disgust and hurt. Seeing that expression on Amanda's face every time always managed to make the hole in Juniper's heart bigger.

Surprisingly, seeing Amanda and Dimitri together didn't make her feel as revolted as she had always been since the beginning of their friendship. Maybe it was because she saw less and less of them throughout the week that followed the highlighted dramatic events. But in all honesty, they looked good as a couple. They proved that stereotypes didn't exist and they looked at each other like they looked at no one. She was not entirely over Dimitri - how could she when all her life she had been pining after him very certain that he was the guy for her? But she accepted the fact that he would never look at her the way she wanted him to, the way he looked at Amanda.

Mr Remirez was arrested for physical abuse and assault. Juniper didn't know the length of his punishment and she wasn't willing to dig herself into another pit hole while she was already struggling to get out of the many that she had already created recently. All she knew was that he was locked up somewhere far away that put enough distance between him and Dimitri. She did care that she hurt Dimitri when she reported his father but she was not the least bit regretful. She was proud of what she did because even though Dimitri couldn't see it - he was blinded by love - she knew what she did was right and that Dimitri would realise the favour she did for him. She just wasn't sure if realisation was going to strike Dimitri Remirez soon or ten years into the future. With the way he was ignoring she simply could not tell.

Dimitri was taken in by Mr and Mrs Helburg who held close relations with the Remirez family before everything in the Remirez family had gone downhill. Juniper wasn't told but she could see by the sour expression he wore every day he departed school to his new residence that he was not pleased. Over the week, however, his grumpy mood lightened and with each day that passed he didn't seem to mind the situation as much as the previous day.

Amanda never bothered to give Juniper a second look. Charlie just snarled or rolled his eyes in utter disgust if he ever saw her. And Dimitri. Dimitri avoided Juniper at all costs. Their friendship wasn't the same ever since she pulled that risky stunt and it ended shortly after Juniper did Dimitri one of the most biggest favours. Weirdly enough, Juniper didn't regret the kiss. It showed that she was human, frail and full of flaws despite what people perceived her to be. She learnt from recent events that life was not always fair and she wasn't going to always be right. She wasn't going to get all that her heart desired and she was bound to stumble and fall a couple of times along her journey of life. But she should get up. Be strong and have courage. Be herself.

Charlie's words had gotten inside her head and she found herself replaying them repeatedly over in her head. He was harsh but his words had definitely hit home. He was right; she was a fraud.

But no more. She wasn't going to act like a fake and be someone she truly wasn't. She was going to be herself. She was going to be Juniper Stauff.

Charlie was quite content. The humiliation had yet to die down but it lessened over the week. He got the chance to ask the girl of his dreams out and while she second doubted their relationship, Charlie was happy that what Juniper did didn't leave such a huge scar behind. It would heal over time surely and this whole fiasco would die down. To anyone who actually thought he was gay he didn't give a shit about. He said that being gay wasn't a problem, it was just the truth behind it and the truth was that Charlie Cox fancied the pants off of the opposite gender only. He did get the attention of a few guys over the week and even Charlie couldn't deny that he was highly flattered.

But he still hadn't forgiven Juniper. And she was about done with all this awkwardness between her and her friends. She wanted her life to be lively again, she wanted her most dearest and closest friends back with her. And she finally embraced the fact that if she wasn't going to do anything then the tension would still continue.

And that thoughts was what lead her to call her mother and tell her that she would be late despite being grounded. She told her mother that he only had an errand to run and that she wouldn't take long. Her mother's protests didn't stop Juniper from going to Charlie Cox's house.

She stood on the doorstep breathing heavily. She came up with numerous scenarios in her head and she played out every possibility. After standing on the porch, idle, for over ten minutes she finally mustered up the courage to ring the bell.

She danced from foot to foot in anticipation before the door opened a couple of seconds later. She froze when her eyes raked over the tall, handsome, blonde haired boy before her eyes. "Juniper Stauff," he said in astonishment. "I thought that I'd never see you again." His blonde hair fell over his alluring eyes and his mouth curved up into a pleasing smile that made her stomach to a small flip.

The boy that stood before her was not Charlie Cox. It was his brother. "Jeremy?" she breathed questionably.

CHAPTER 14

3 years ago

The first time Juniper Stauff met Jeremy Cox she wasn't entirely impressed nor was she pleased with his rather exotic character.

Charlie had missed a day of school and Juniper decided she would take the responsibility of delivering his homework to him as well as Mrs Monroe's threat on his overdue assignments. She had stood on the porch of the Cox's household and rang the bell after collecting her breath. A cheery smile immediately took over her lips when she saw the door open to reveal a tall, lean boy. He had unruly blond curls that fell over his dark, hauntingly captivating brown eyes and a very forlorn expression on his face.

Juniper's greeting had died down in her throat once she got an overall look of the boy that stood before her, his figure towering high above her. He looked older than her but she couldn't exactly tell his age. God knows what age he was. She wasn't a mind-reader.

She quickly gathered herself and the cheery smile was back on her face as fast as a lightening bolt that it seemed like her smile had not faltered when in actual fact it had. "Hi," she chirped, smiling wider as she greeted the stranger.

"Uh, hey," he replied, his deep voice sounding groggy like he had just woken up from sleep. "What do you want?"

She tried her best to keep the smile on her face and not flinch at how clipped his voice sounded. She definitely did not approve of the tone he used on her, especially when she had greeted him in such a lovely way.

"I stopped by to give this to Charlie," she had said as she held out her hand and handed over the papers to the boy that stood before her.

"Why?"

"Because he wasn't in school." Confusion laced her voice before realisation struck her. Charlie had probably ditched school.

"That bastard," the boy muttered under his breath.

She looked at him as curiosity bubbled at high levels within her. "So you're Charlie's brother?" she asked as she quirked an inquisitive brow.

"Yes, Jeremy Cox."

Juniper's eyes sparkled with interest. "How come I've never seen you at school?"

"That's because I go to Dixton High."

"That's amazing. Have you seen Jennifer Varson? She's my cousin."

"Uh, yeah, probably." He gave Juniper a weird look, one mixed with interest and annoyance. She wondered how that was even possible.

"So how old are you?" she asked, her eyes sparkling with interest. Clearly her fifteen year old self didn't know that as she asked these questions she sounded like a total creeper.

"Why is that important?" His glare was accusing.

She shrugged, her curiosity sinking back by the slightest bit. "I was just curious," she whispered in a low voice.

"Eighteen."

"You're three years older than me-"

"Yeah. I'll tell Charlie you dropped by." And with that he shut the door right in her face, not even allowing her a moment to tell him her name.

How rude, she thought.

The second time Juniper Stauff met Jeremy Cox she was concerned and slightly agitated.

She had usually gone to the beach on weekends. Beyond the boulder of rocks that were situated on the far side of the beach was her small little sanctuary that she went to every weekend in the night, creeping out of the house and spending endless hours watching the scenery before her and thinking about everything she had and everything she didn't have. One misfortunate Wednesday Mr and Mrs Stauff were fighting and her parents rarely fought. When they did it was either to tease the other or they were extremely mad. By the octave of their voices Juniper knew it wasn't right for her to intrude when her parents were clearly sorting out some unresolved issues. It didn't help when she needed to study and all she could hear were their loud, booming voices penetrating through the walls in the house. She understood that couples always fought but did they have to fight in the middle of her mid-terms? That didn't sound the slightest bit fair on her case.

She had tucked a few books into her bag and slung it over her shoulder, walking down the steps of the staircase in her house soft as a mouse. As soon as she was out the door, she darted to the beach which wasn't far from her house. She needed a peaceful place to study and clear out the whirlwind of worrisome thoughts of her parents that consumed her mind.

When she had arrived at her sanctuary she was taken by surprise. She wasn't the only one who knew that this beautiful place existed beyond the boulder of rocks.

"Jeremy?" she asked as she neared the figure who was clad all in black. She was hesitant in calling out his name because she wasn't sure if that was his name. She didn't have the best memory and she'd only met him once. She didn't think that their first memory was of importance. She had no idea what it would lead to then.

The figure turned towards her and she shrieked when she noticed how dark his gaze was. He held a bottle in one hand as he swayed with the wind. His drunken gaze landed on Juniper and she suddenly felt stripped of the peace that she sought. "Oh, it's you, that girl," he said, his lips curling into a snarl as his words mashed over each other.

She tried her very best not to frown. Why did he seem so rude? "Uh, Juniper," she said, looking at him through her lashes afraid that if she looked him directly in the eyes, his gaze would smother her.

"What?" he asked rather rudely, dipping his head back and pouring some of the contents of the bottle into his mouth.

She had taken slow and careful steps towards the boy until she was standing in front of him. "My name is Juniper. Juniper Stauff."

"Strange name," he commented, his voice void of emotion.

She forced a laugh, slightly nervous with his presence. "Yeah, most people just call me June. I was born in June anyway," she said forcing a light hearted chuckle. But with the heavy and dark atmosphere that cloaked them, Jeremy could tell that she was not comfortable with his presence.

"The irony. Quite amusing," he replied, his sentences and voice clipped. He didn't laugh nor did he look the least bit amused.

"You have a funny way of expressing your emotions." The words had escaped her mouth unwillingly and she froze as his dark gaze settled back on her.

His lips tipped up, a flickering smile appearing for a second before it disappeared and he took another swig of his bottle to cover his slip. "I've been told, Juniper."

The third time that Juniper Stauff met Jeremy Cox she wished that she hadn't stumbled upon his existence for he gave her a memory that was frightening and she never knew she could feel like this way towards a person who she had only met twice.

It was one of those weekend evenings when the sun was just about to set, the gloomy clouds loomed over and the winds whistled. She often found herself in the sanctuary at these sort of times over the weekend. When she went to the sanctuary she was surprised to see that Jeremy Cox was there. She certainly wasn't as surprised as the first time she spot him in her sanctuary but she was still in shock.

Jeremy stood still, swaying at the howling wind's will. Ugly tears flowed down his face, his stubble looked damp and he looked a mess. In his left hand he held an empty beer bottle and in his right hand, he held onto a pocket knife, the blade shining brilliantly under the disappearing sun rays.

"Jeremy," she gasped as she rushed to his aid.

"Get away from me," he pushed her away and in result of the force he ended up staggering back a little. The fact that he was drunk didn't help his footing.

"Are you okay?" she asked, concerned.

"Absolutely fine," he snapped. "What are you doing here?"

"Well," she said, gulping breaths of air. The nervousness had settled in her stomach and it didn't help that his drunken gaze seemed to be burning holes into her. "This is my, um, sanctuary."

"Find another sanctuary tonight!" His voice held an edge of urgency and Juniper furrowed her brows as she took a cautious step forward.

"What's got you in a mood?" she asked. She was about done with his unthoughtful behaviour towards her despite their short, little meetings. "What's wrong with you? Have your parents not taught you manners?" she questioned, momentarily forgetting that the Cox family had lost their father a few prior to their third meeting.

His tired eyes met hers. "I don't have a father."

Guilt immediately took over her. "I-I for-forgot," she stuttered, embarrassed and ashamed.

His eyes trained on her before he sighed, dropping the bottle. It hit the hard ground, the soft thud echoed through the somber evening. "I'm leaving," he said, his words sounded awfully cryptic as his grasp tightened around the pocket knife which resulted in his knuckles turning paler.

"Why?"

He looked at her then, his eyes not guarded as it had been in their two previous meetings. "I have nothing else to lose," he whispered so softly that she had to strain her ears and step closer to him to hear the words.

She caught onto the words and her heart twisted at the tone of his voice. "What about your mum and Charlie? And you're friends?"

"I don't have friends," he said, only addressing the second question and avoiding the first.

"You can't leave them," she said, her heart suddenly softening up to the rude boy. "They are your family–"

"I have nothing to live for anymore."

His words sliced through the wind and summoned a sort of pity and shock that Juniper had never felt before. His words caused an abrupt silence in the evening. Even the wind had stopped whistling.

"You can't say that," she said quietly as she searched his face. This was the first time she wasn't hesitant or nervous or the slightest bit afraid to look him directly in the eye. But his mask was up soon as he let her catch a glimpse of his battling emotions.

"I can say whatever the hell I please to say," he lashed out. "Now please go."

But she didn't move from her post. "Listen, how about we go back to your house and you and your family can sort things out."

He stared at her, momentarily mesmerized by her character. They barely knew each other yet she seemed to care for him so much more than his 'friends' ever did after his father's passing. It was a while before he replied, his gaze on her suddenly calculating.

"Fine," he huffed. "You go ahead. I'll, uh, catch up with you. I just need a moment."

Juniper looked at him dubiously, her eyes moving her the knife that he gripped at. Something told her that he wasn't telling the truth and he was holding something back. She didn't want to push her luck so despite her strong gut feeling she put on a smile and pushed aside that feeling that seemed to grow bigger by the second. "Sure," she breathed as she decided that he had earned his space.

She turned her back to him, walked a bit before she had begun climbing the rocks to get to the other side. The cold wind whipped around her body and she clung to the rocks, a slight spasm of panic hitting her. Catching her balance, she took a deep breath and looked up at the dizzy blue sky.

And then everything happened so fast.

A shattering scream pierced the still evening, taking Juniper completely by surprise. The grip she had on the rocks loosened due to the jolt of her body when she heard the scream. She lost her footing and reached out desperately to clung onto the rocks but the hard, scrapy surface barely bruised her skin as she fell backwards, her foot slipping off the rock and her arms flailing in the air. The fall was short, lasting for less than a second for she hadn't climbed a lot but when she felt the hard ground beneath her after the loud thud resonated in her ears, she moaned when she tried to move. A jolt of pain shot up her abdomen and spine and she bit back the stinging tears as she tried to sit up.

When she cast her eyes elsewhere in search for the scream she caught sight of Jeremy and a horrifying scream instantly left her lips, emerging from the depths of her throat and piercing the evening with a fearful, horrendous noise. Jeremy Cox was on his knees, his left hand wound around the pocket knife that was no longer by his side but in his body. The end of the pocket knife protruded from his chest and blood covered his hands and everything that Jeremy laid a finger on. His shallow screaming dimmed the longer he held tighter to the knife.

Juniper recovered fast from her shock and scrambled to her feet, wincing immediately when a shot of pain attacked her midsection. She ignored the stinging pain in her ribs as she dragged herself to Jeremy's body, trying her best to subside her own pain so she could help another.

Jeremy's face paled all at once, his grip around this pocket knife loosened and his hand fell back down to his side. His attractive, drunken, dark brown eyes dimmed as his face crumbled and he fell, face first into the ground.

Juniper shrieked and willed the forceful sobs down her throat. She was not going to cry when she had to help him. But as she slowly turned his heavy body around so that his face was now facing her, sobs erupted from deep within her chest. He had a blank look in his eyes like he was long gone and she quickly reached for his throat, not giving up on her hope too quickly. With a tear streaked face and shaking hands, her fingers searched for a pulse and when she didn't find any, the tears poured down faster and heavier. Her hand turned neither warm nor cold when she held in over his mouth. She looked at his chest and saw that the pocket knife was not pierced into his heart, but slightly below it. It didn't seem like the right position for his heart and with a sudden, blossoming courage and strength, she swallowed down her sobs and turned to the dying boy in need of her help.

She gripped the knife and with quite some forceful work and strength on her end, she managed to take the knife out and almost instantly, blood started flowing out from the stabbed area. She grabbed his shirt and ripped off majority of the thin material with the help of the bloody pocket knife. Working around his body, by lifting him up every few seconds so she could slip the material under him, she wrapped the material around his chest to help reduce the blood flow and apply pressure on his wound.

She wasted no time. Her trembling hands moved to her jeans and she pulled out her phone, fumbling with it as her shaking hands only grew more shakier. She called the emergency number and when most of the situation seemed to be solved and there was nothing else she could do, she cast her gaze down to the dying boy and she made the mistake of looking down at herself and all the horror that sat before her.

Blood.

It was everywhere and it was all she could see. Panic swelled from the depths of her chest and rose to her throat, the sudden lack of oxygen making her shake and tremble even more. Blotches of black entered her vision as her head throbbed with an unbearable pain. She tried to get rid of the pain but she couldn't. This was what happened when she saw blood; she had hemophobia.

When she was fixing Jeremy, she was too engrossed in helping save a life and she was too panicked to even recognise the blood but now that she was conscious of the blood that was splayed everywhere, her mind whirling and reality slipping from her grasp... It wasn't too long before her body hit the hard, cold ground, beside Jeremy, and darkness swallowed her whole.

CHAPTER 15

J uniper Stauff and Jeremy Cox stared at each other for a couple more seconds, their surprised expressions shown clearly on their faces.

Seconds later, Jeremy Cox collected her small body and hugged her. He barely knew the girl yet he missed her. It was her act of bravery that had saved him and he would be forever in debt to her. She stopped him from doing a ruthless, horrible thing and he couldn't have been more happy to see his saviour right in front of his eyes after three long years.

Juniper stiffened before she felt herself relaxing. She wound her arms around his waist, buried her head into his chest and welcomed the warmth of his embrace.

Juniper had only hugged Jeremy twice. The first time she hugged him was the day he was released from the hospital. She had stayed over at the hospital after she was medically attended to and she visited the hospital each day, spending endless hours on her phone as she waited for the boy she saved to be discharged. He was in a critical condition when the ambulance had come to pick him up and Juniper only found out this information after she awoke from her blackout. And because Juniper wasn't part of family she was not permitted to see him. So the second he was discharged she ran to him and hugged the living daylights out of him. He was highly surprised and mildly amused by the sudden action, she remembered, but he had soon caved into the affection and hugged her back.

The second time she hugged him was when she went over to the Cox's household to tutor Charlie in History because he was failing and she needed the credits. It was the day that Jeremy was leaving to the rehabilitation centre to get better and overcome his depression. Seeing his mother and younger brother looking devastated with tears in their eyes moved her and she soon was so caught up in the moment that she embarrassingly opened her arms and asked for a hug.

Standing here in Jeremy's arms it surprised her by how vividly she remembered such little details which she had deemed insignif-icant in her life. She had pushed all memories of Jeremy away when he was sent off three years ago. When she pulled back she looked at him with a dazed sort of look in her eyes.

"You look like you can't believe what you're seeing," he said, his familiar lips turning up into a familiar smirk.

It was surprisingly shocking and slightly refreshing to see him like this. The three encounters Juniper shared with Jeremy, he was anything but kind. He was cold-hearted and downright rude, always having that venomous look in his eyes. The Jeremy Cox that stood before her didn't look like the Jeremy Cox she knew of - not that she actually knew him well. He looked different; eyes sparking; lips smiling.

"It's really you," she breathed unbelievingly, a smile taking over her lips.

He chuckled at her reaction. Apologizing for his lack of manners - which wasn't what the old Jeremy Cox would say - he opened the door and gestured her in. If possible, Juniper's wide smile widened as she stepped into the house.

"I actually came here to see Charlie," she said as she turned back to face Jeremy. "Is he home?"

He looked at her and for a second Juniper recognised him. Jeremy's eyes turned cold and his smile disappeared. "He's upstairs," he replied and after a paused, he added, "you two fought, didn't you?" His eyes held curiosity but they were also mixed with a blaze of anger.

"Yeah," she replied softly as she fidgeted with her fingers. "I did something to him. Something that I shouldn't have done." She looked into Jeremy's eyes, determination settling within her as she spoke the next few words. "I can't take the silent treatment anymore and I thought I should apologize."

"I know what happened."

She stilled. "What?" Juniper was taken aback by his words.

"I know what you 'supposedly' did to Charlie," he said as he used air-quotations. "I kind of am angry at you for taking the blame but you're not the person I should be angry at since you didn't do this to him. Why are you taking the blame?"

She stared at him, mouth agape as she tried to decipher how he knew this much about her. Obviously Charlie told him about this issue but Charlie thought it was all Juniper's doing so how did Jeremy see through that lie? "No," she started as she regained her composure, "it was my fault."

But Jeremy didn't buy her lies. "Look, I may not know you as well as Charlie knows you or your other friends know you but I do know that you're a kind, brave girl who will do whatever it takes to get her happiness. Hurting my little brother doesn't seem like something you would do-"

That's where you're wrong about me, she thought bitterly to herself.

"-Why else would you call an ambulance and save me, not leaving me to die and rot there?"

"Maybe because that's what any sane and sensible person would have done," she offered, her voice holding an underlying tone of defence. She didn't want to expose Dimitri. Their wrecked friendship was already too much for her to handle.

"Not if that sane person has a blackout at the mere sight of blood. You tried to reduce the blood flow and keep me alive. Not many people would do that, be it they have phobia or not. So I'm not arguing with the fact that you are sane. I'm just trying to figure out why you're lying to Charlie. He seems pretty convinced that some other boy did this to him with your aid. Is what you're protecting worth breaking off your friendship with my brother?"

Juniper gulped as she felt Jeremy's dark gaze upon her. She had never felt this vulnerable - excluding the party in Brooke's where she almost got raped. Nobody ever saw through her that fast - not even Dimitri. And this had begun to scare her.

Jeremy sighed when he realised that he wasn't going to get a reply out of the blonde-haired girl. He leaned against the doorframe, his dark gaze upon her calculating. It was that same look he had on when he almost committed suicide, when she had offered him a ride home to settle all his thoughts and doubts with his mother and brother. This look made her heart drop. What was he thinking?

"Do you remember that promise you told me about?" he asked slowly like he was trying his level best to crack an unbreakable code. "At the hospital when I was discharged I asked you why you helped me. And you said-"

She finished off his sentence for him as a feeling of nostalgia took over her and staring into his intoxicatingly charming brown eyes made her feel as if she was under some sort of trance. "-I said that I made a promise to myself when I was a small girl. I promised to help everyone and bring peace and bliss into their lives. I was willing to save anyone that I was able to save."

Her eyes began to prick with tears as a lump formed in her throat. She had promised herself. And look what she had done. She was so caught up in the moment she shared with Jeremy that she was oblivious to the figure that stood a few feet behind her, hidden against the wall, listening to Juniper's and Jeremy's entire conversation with rapt attention.

"I thought I could be a superhero," she whispered at last.

"You're not much of one, are you?" came a familiar deep voice from behind her and she jolted in surprise, startled at the new voice.

She turned around and her face paled when she came face to face with Charlie Cox. A deafening silence followed and Juniper's heart beat loud in her chest, slamming against her ribcage every few seconds.

"Okay then," Jeremy said as he clasped his hands together. His voice caused a crack on the thin ice that had settled into the living room. "I guess I'll leave you two to it." With an awkward parting he left, "adios amigos."

In a swift motion he was out of the room and Charlie and Juniper were left in a very awkward situation.

It was Charlie this time who broke the silence. "Why are you here, June? Have you come to see my brother?" His tone held an edge of hostility to it.

"I didn't know he was out of-"

"Cut the crap," Charlie interjected as his face turned sour. You read the letter, didn't you?" He looked at Juniper and she knew that he was seeing just how much she was willing to lie to him so instead of denying his accusation, she diverted the topic.

"Look," she started, "I didn't come here to pick a fight. I want you back as my friend and I came here to apologize for the shitty inconveniences that I may have caused you."

He gave her a long, calculating stare - not much different from the one Jeremy gave her and she momentarily found herself wondering if it was in the Cox's nature to always be this suspicious and cautious. He finally sighed and jerked his head to the side motioning her to follow him. He lead her into the kitchen and offered her a seat on one of the stools that sat still by the kitchen counter.

Opening the fridge, he asked, "would you like anything to drink?"

Juniper was taken aback by his sudden hospitality. One minute he was hostile and the next he was hospitable. "Uh, sure," she replied. "What do you have?"

"Um," he said as he buried his head behind the door of the fridge. "Fanta, Pepsi, Beer and oh, mum made fresh orange juice."

"Orange juice please," she smiled. She was not a fan of soft, fizzy drinks. Fresh juice, on the other hand, was always refreshing.

He opened up one of the top cupboards and pulled out a long, narrow glass. Pouring orange juice into the glass, he slid it to her and left the jug on her counter next to her seat in case she wanted to help herself to more juice.

She smiled at him after taking one long gulp of the fresh orange juice. "Mhm, thanks," she beamed up at him as he came to take a seat on the stool beside hers. "This tastes amazing."

"Yeah," he mumbled giving her a sideways glance. "I'll be sure to tell mum that."

"You should," she replied, enthusiastically. "How is she doing?"

When no reply came, she looked up from her glass of orange juice only to see a hostile expression on Charlie's face. It looked rather odd since she barely saw him with that expression on his face. "Right," she said after the pause in their conversation. The juice was so divine that she almost forgot the reason she came to see Charlie in the first place. But before Juniper could get a word out of her mouth, Charlie asked, "Why?"

"Excuse me?" Juniper said, a little startled and confused with the direction of his question.

"Why are you defending Dimitri?"

"He didn't do anything, Charlie!" she burst. "I did. I was the one who suggested that he should take revenge and I should help him. It's my fault really. Even if he was the one to put up those pictures, it was me - damn it, I could have stopped him. But I didn't because my heart wanted more than it could have."

"You just admitted that Dimitri was part of this," he replied curtly.

She felt a little breathless after her mini-rant and she gave out a huff of breath, blowing away a stray piece of her blonde hair that obstructed her view. A couple days ago, she dyed her hair back to blonde because she missed how she looked in the light colour. She was really indecisive when it came down to her hair.

When she didn't deny Charlie's statement, he said, "I guess we learn new things everyday, don't we?" He tilted his head to the side and he tried to see what it was about Juniper that his brother, Jeremy, felt attracted to. Frankly, he couldn't see the beauty his brother saw for all Charlie saw after the recent events was a dark soul. His vision of her was now tainted, not the same as it once was.

"I'm sorry, Charlie. I just...I thought...oh gosh, I'm sorry Charlie," she gushed, her eyes filling with tears. She didn't know how the phrase her emotions and that was frustrating her. What was wrong with her? Recent events had broke down her walls. She turned away so Charlie couldn't see her face.

"I, uh, I better get going," she said and she stood so abruptly that her stool feel over.

Could she get any more clumsier? Her cheeks tainted with pink as she pulled the stool back up and gave Charlie a tight-lipped smile.

"Apology accepted," he said, his lips lifting up into a brief smile. "I'll walk you out."

Charlie led Juniper to the door and leaned against the doorframe when Juniper looked up at him with a questioning look in her eyes. "I thought you wouldn't forgive me," she admitted.

"I'm not going to see you the way I've always seen you. You and I both know you're not as innocent as you claim to be. I should have guessed that a person cannot be all good because they have to have a little evil in them. Yours is selfishness instead of the selfless person you pretend to be."

Juniper's heart swelled with pain. Was this what Dimitri also thought about her now? Was that what everybody who knew of her dirty deeds thought of her? Was that what everybody would think if they were all to know the truth? Then she looked up to him a said, "will you hurt Dimitri?"

"As long as you don't hurt my big brother, I wouldn't lay a finger on Remirez," Charlie said, his gaze holding a threatening look to it.

"What?" Her heart did a small jump at Charlie's words.

"For some whacked up reason my brother seems to like you. Maybe it was because without you he wouldn't be here. You hurt him and I will kill you, June." With one wry smile, Charlie turned on his heel and shut the door behind him.

Juniper Stauff stood on the porch for a full minute, her legs unable to move her to her car. Why was it that Charlie's words warmed her heart? Jeremy liked her and through all the horrible things she went through with all her loved ones turning their backs on her, it was nice to know that someone took a liking to her - be it a person she barely even knew.

Looks like Juniper had herself a new friend. All she had to do now was get his number.

CHAPTER 16

Apologising was one of the toughest things Juniper Stauff had ever ever done. It certainly didn't help when the people she wanted to apologise to avoided her like she was the plague.

Every time Amanda Obereen spotted Juniper approaching her, she would turn around and walk away. It stung Juniper a little that Amanda was ignoring her and giving her the cold shoulder. Over the week that her most beloved friends decided to ignore her and treat her like she was not there, like she wore some sort of invisibility cloak over her, she had plenty of time to think of her relationships with them.

She only started to despise Amanda when Dimitri started dating her and maybe it was jealousy that caused her to hate Amanda. Now, almost friendless, Juniper realised she missed Amanda's company. She was blinded by what she assumed to be love that she couldn't see what Amanda and her friendship was worth.

Juniper was going to stop being blinded by things that had the capability to wreck her life. She was going to right her wrongs and prove to Charlie, and mostly herself, that she was not a fraud.

Finally, after a week with putting up with all of this, Juniper cornered Amanda in the girls' locker room of the gymnasium. The smell of sweat mixed with deodorant filled her nostrils and she tried to puke from the horrendous smell of the place. She was here to apologise. Better get it over with before the horrid odour got to her head and she started to hallucinate.

"June," Amanda said, her eyes guarded and her expression stony.

"Hey Mandy," Juniper smiled in attempt to lighten the mood. Seeing as Amanda's scowl only deepened with her rigid attitude, it was clear as day that Juniper's smile wasn't working as it usually did in their conversations. Juniper sighed, the smile that graced her lips thinned. "Listen, I'm sorry-"

"What's done is done. It's in the past." Giving Juniper one last blank look, she turned on her heel and and pushed past Juniper so she could make her exit.

But Juniper was determined to earn Amanda's forgiveness. She yearned to feel the love and care that their friendship provided. She gripped Amanda's wrist and brought her to a halt. Turning around, Amanda threw her hands into the air in exasperation. "What do you want from me, June?"

The girls that were in the process of changing turned their head towards Juniper and Amanda when they heard Amanda's exclamation. Amanda lowered her hands to her sides when she noticed the sudden attention on her and her cheeks flushed pink in embarrassment. "Um," Juniper said as she diverted her attention from the curious stares the girls were giving Amanda. "Can we please go somewhere else."

Amanda gave her a three second stare before she rolled her eyes in a rude manner. "Fine," she replied somewhat reluctantly. "Lead the way." Juniper tried not to flinch at the tone that was being used on her. Amanda had never treated Juniper this way.

I deserve it though, Juniper thought as she led Amanda out of the girls' locker room and into the vacant corridor. Most people were in class now and it was their gym period but their teacher was absent and there was no substitute teacher either.

"I'm sorry," Juniper said once again when they got away from the mass of gossiping girls.

"I thought you were a nice girl," Amanda bit out getting straight to the point. "You were always a wonderful friend. What on earth did I do to you to make you do this to me?"

"I didn't mean to. I was just - I'm sorry." There was not much Juniper could say. All she could say was that she was sorry. She, however, wanted to say more that just sorry but at that moment words failed her as they often did and she had not a clue of how to phrase her emotions into words. English was never her speciality anyway.

"Saying sorry over and over again doesn't make up for what you did. Do you know how embarrassing it was to turn up to school smelling like tuna and have cold, hardened egg goo stuck to my hair? I tried everything to get rid of the stink and tried washing my hair like a madwoman to get the egg out of my hair. I only managed to look less worse when I came to school. That didn't stop everybody from stepping away and keeping a five mile radius from me. They were ignoring me like I was..." Amanda took a deep breath in the middle of her rant as she searched for the word to finish her sentence.

"Like you were the plague?" Juniper suggested, her voice low and knowing. She knew how it felt to be in Amanda's position. She was currently in Amanda's position.

An icy glare was sent to Juniper. "Are you mocking me, Juniper Anne Stauff?"

"No, no, no," Juniper gushed. "I was...oh, well, nevermind. I was just jealous." At this point she had begun to play with the hem of her shirt, embarrassment tinting her cheeks as she looked down to the floor. Wow, the floor looks super shiny today, she thought.

"Jealous?" Amanda echoed. "What would you be jealous of?"

Juniper hesitantly lifted her head up to look Amanda in the eye. Confusion was written on the both the girls faces. Had Dimitri not told Amanda about Juniper's infatuation towards him? And why not? Weren't couples supposed to tell each other the truth and not hide anything from each other?

Juniper thought that exposing herself and Dimitri in the process would only cause the wedge between them to grow bigger and so she decided to take opportunity of the situation.

"Well," she started. "You guys are the perfect couple. You have what I don't have. You two are love partners, you know that the other person loves you back. I guess that was what made me so jealous..." All the confidence that Juniper had about two seconds ago instantly deflated once she opened her mouth. She might have not been telling Amanda the truth but she surely wasn't lying.

Dropping her voice by just a notch she looked past Amanda - at anything that was not Amanda Obereen. "Society didn't hold you back. He was at the bottom of the social ladder while you were at the very top. You two never let that interfere with the relationship that you two shared. Why? I didn't understand at first but recent events showed me something. They showed me that love existed, that you two truly do love each other and when love happens, it hits you so hard that all you see is the shadow; that there is a light at the end of the tunnel; that you have a saviour."

She looked up to see Amanda staring at her with mild confusion written clearly across her face. But there was another look on her face - understanding. Amanda knew exactly what Juniper's words meant and she knew that Juniper liked Dimitri. It wasn't that hard to tell in all honesty. "You're Juniper Stauff. You can get any guy that you want," Amanda said.

"Not when the guy you want doesn't think of you the way that you think of him," Juniper said, smiling through the piercing pain that shot suddenly at her heart. She had repeatedly told herself that she didn't like Dimitri anymore but it was going to take more than just a week to rid this emotion.

"I still don't get it," Amanda said. "Why..?"

Juniper faced Amanda, dropping her façade for a minute so that Amanda so she could tell Amanda as much truth as she was able to. "You hurt him, Mandy," she said. And I made you hurt him, she thought bitterly about herself. "He is the closest friend I have ever had and if you saw just how much he looked broken and hurt...I was desperate to make him feel better. I couldn't let him go on beating himself down like that. I had to do something-"

"Taking revenge on me was your solution?"

"He's my friend, Amanda, and he doesn't seem like my best friend now because he's ignoring me like all of you are but would you not do something similar if you were in my shoes?" Juniper didn't tell the truth, she manipulated it so she could return to her old life. Juniper Stauff was desperate.

"No."

For a moment Juniper was stunned by Amanda's response.

"I would do far worse," Amanda said before cracking a smile. Juniper ignored the hesitance of the smile and accepted it anyway. "I'm sorry avoiding you like-"

"The plague?" Juniper suggested but this time in an entirely different mood set. Juniper's remark sent the two girls into fits of laughter.

When their laughter died down, Amanda said, "why didn't you tell me that you liked Dimitri? I would have backed off. Now I won't but maybe if you told me before I would have stepped away."

Juniper shrugged. "That's over. You two belong with each other and you definitely have my blessing," she smiled, winking teasily at the end.

"Apology accepted," Amanda grinned but Juniper clearly say that the grin was anything but sincere. Then she looked sideways at her old friend and with a mischievous spark in her eyes, she asked, "want to bunk class and head for ice cream instead?"

"Like old times?" Juniper smirked making it seem that they hadn't done this in forever as her heart fluttered with hope. Maybe their friendship wasn't all that broken as she thought.

Amanda rolled her eyes and looped her dark arm through Juniper's and dragged her out of the school. "We'll have time to talk about how stupid your revenge plan was." Juniper tried to ignore the fact that Amanda had just dodged the bullet. It certainly was not going to be like old times.

Juniper giggled, trying to keep her fake excitement and happiness evident on her face, just like her old self would have done.

Arm in arm, the giggling girls emerged into the open, fresh air. As they headed to the ice-cream shop in Amanda's car Juniper let her worries slip away for the briefest of time. Things weren't right with Amanda but at least she had fixed a part of it, at least she had gotten the forgiveness she wanted.

She'd yet to have to think of a way to approach Dimitri without embarrassing herself. If only falling out of love was simple as falling into it.

Chapter 17

Ever since Dimitri Remirez got back with Amanda Obereen he never left her side. No, he wasn't clingy. He was just trying to stay well away from Juniper. However, when Juniper's and Amanda's friendship was reignited, it got harder and harder for Dimitri to avoid Juniper. Every time he saw her he would think of what she'd done but over the week he had a lot of time to think to himself and he realised what Juniper had accused of his father's monstrosity was true.

Juniper was sick and tired of the cold shoulder she received from Dimitri. She'd often laid on her bed as she stared at the ceiling and mulled over their good times together. Why had she kissed him? What on earth was she thinking when she did that? She had known how Dimitri felt yet she let her emotions get the better of her by thinking that in all this sadness he might respond. She scoffed at herself as she thought of how desperate Dimitri must have thought she was. She couldn't be more embarrassed of herself.

And even though she was tired of taking all the blame, she couldn't bring herself to confront Dimitri and ask for forgiveness like she had done Charlie and Amanda. She had overstepped her limits with Dimitri and asking for forgiveness from him was not only frightening but it didn't seem right after all she had put him through.

So she waited. She waited until he realised what sort of person his father was and if her action against his father was for the better or for the worse. After all, Juniper had done all this for him because she cared for him more than a friend should.

It was two weeks before graduation when Dimitri finally accepted the fact that his father was locked up for his benefit and decided that he needed to fix things with Juniper - or at least talk to her.

"Hey," he said somewhat awkwardly as he stood behind her as she exchanged books through her locker.

She turned around hesitantly and looked at him for a few seconds, her heart beating rapidly within the confinements of her chest. "Hello," she replied.

"We need to talk."

She nodded and a smile easily slipped onto her pink lips. "What's up?"

"How about we head for ice-cream. School's over so, um, we talk over ice-cream..?"

"Sure," she said without thinking twice. She couldn't help but think about how Amanda had suggested the same thing. Had Dimitri and Amanda talked about Juniper and all the horrible things she was trying to make up to?

"Great!" He sounded relieved. "Can we take your car? My car-"

"Existed centuries ago," she finished, nudging his shoulder teasingly.

An all too familiar smile slipped onto his adorable features. "Oh, shut up," he groaned rolling his eyes. He was trying to give some sort of annoyed vibe to Juniper but his smile didn't help his situation.

"That's something the Great Juniper Stauff is incapable of doing," Juniper smiled deviously as she put her hands on her hips and thrust her chin up in mock pride.

A laugh erupted from Dimitri's mouth and it wasn't until he laughed out loud did she realise that she missed his laugh. "Come on," he said and slipped his hand into hers before pulling her out the school doors.

Juniper didn't understand how one minute they were fighting and the next moment conversation flowed easily between them. Maybe it was because they were once best friends and that gave them all the more reason to converse with the other but maybe it was also a longing for the relationship they shared; a friendship so unique and beautiful.

"Oh my, this chocolate fudge ice-cream is amazing!" she moaned as she closed her eyes and let the milky, soft ice-cream dissolve and do wonders in her mouth.

"Vanilla tastes so much better," Dimitri argued.

Before Dimitri could do anything, Juniper leaned over their table and nipped at his ice-cream, letting the flavour dissolve on her tongue. This was something she and Dimitri had always done but it had become a lost tradition. A milky moustache had formed on her upper lip as she beamed at Dimitri, victory written clear across her face.

"Nah, I beg to differ," she smiled. "This chocolate fudge tastes much better than plain vanilla."

Juniper thought Dimitri looked rather weird as she took a look at his reaction. He had his lips pressed tightly together, his face growing a little red. Then it hit her. He was trying not to laugh.

"Oh no," she said as she removed the tissue from around her wafer cone and wiped her lips with it. "Why does this happen to me so often?"

Dimitri burst into fits of laughter, his face more red that it almost matched the colour of the jagged scar that ran down his cheek to the tip of his lips. "Oh God, that was priceless," he chuckled, his shoulders bouncing up and down in the process.

"Shut up," she blushed.

"I got to say," Dimitri smirked, "you look handsome with that moustache."

"Oh my, will you just shut up!"

Soon they finished eating their ice-creams, Juniper's embarrassment slowly dying down as they both ate their ice-creams in peaceful silence. The silence had allowed both Dimitri and Juniper to think of a way to approach the subject that had driven a huge rift in one of the most beautiful friendships in Sereneigo.

They both paid for their ice-creams and headed out of the shop. the door giving out a light jingle as the bell sounded off as the door opened and closed. The summer days were drawing to an end, the heat had simmered down and this made Juniper excited. She had always preferred winter to summer. Autumn was her favourite season.

"I had a lovely time," she smiled as she faced Dimitri, pulling her cardigan tighter around her body. "You could come over for dinner tonight if you like! Mum has somehow got it into her head that you're deviously handsome and a ridiculously funny guy. Where she got that idea is beyond me."

Dimitri tucked his hands into his pockets, the heavy air weighed down on them as he stood over Juniper, his lanky body casting a shadow over her figure. "Am I not?" he asked, feigning a hurt expression.

"Yes, mister, you certainly are not," she smirked, amused as raised a teasing brow at her friend trying to fake this as long as she could before the storm was to hit. Enjoy the calm. Face the aftermath later.

"Really? That's not what you thought of me before we got arrested."

His tone was light and humorous and Juniper knew he was only enjoying the calm like she was and avoiding the storm like she was. She knew he didn't mean it anyway that would offend her. But those words. They reminded her that no matter what she tried she could not erase the past; one futile mistake that managed to twist her life.

Juniper had stiffened, the smile slipped off her face. She tried to find a distraction, anything that would help her to stop looking at him.

"June, you know I didn't mean it like that. I was just..." Dimitri sighed then and ran a frustrated hand through his brown, tousled hair. "Oh God, I'm sorry."

Juniper looked up at her supposed best friend. She shook her head and placed her hands into the pocket of her jeans not quite sure of what she should have done with her hands.

"You shouldn't be sorry. I should. Reporting your dad..." she said, looking up at the broken boy. "I was overstepping my boundaries but you got me pissed and I...I couldn't see you like that anymore despite only getting to see you looking like shit only twice. Call it love or care. Call it whatever the hell you want. I just wanted to see my friend happy so I'm sorry for overstepping my boundaries but I am not sorry for reporting your father. Admitting him to a rehabilitation would have been a better idea. I was consumed in my anger that I didn't really give what I was doing a second thought."

Dimitri had refused to look at Juniper as she talked. Then he said, staring down at the gravel ground, "I hated you for what you did. Well, I thought I hated you. I just didn't want you to be right so I made myself hate you for what you did. Mr and Mrs Helburg took me in. They were close with my dad once upon a time. You know, before my dad became a drunken arsehole."

Juniper gasped and that's when Dimitri looked up at her. He smiled faintly but his smile held no humour or amusement. "Yeah, my dad's an arse. It's just... I know I have family. I have you and I have Amanda. But my dad was the only blood family I had left in Sereneigo and I couldn't afford to lose that so I did whatever it took to keep him. First day at the Helburg's house was quiet. I wasn't used to it. I guess, over the week I came to terms with the fact that I liked this; not having to come home worrying about what my father was doing to do to me or what mess I'd have to clean up or a reminder of what I had to live up to."

He smiled again except this time Juniper could see the sincerity behind the smile. "I sat Mr and Mrs Helburg down yesterday and came clean. I told them everything. They even wanted to see my scars but I told them that was for another day. So thank you, June.

Thank you for making me realise who my father is; a monstrous arsehole."

They both chuckled a little at Dimitri's last proclamation and Juniper nodded. There was a quick silence before Juniper sighed. Better now than never, she had thought. "After all the shit that happened, I realised that I didn't love you," she said, biting down on her lips nervously.

"Ouch. An arrow right to the heart," he said, shaking his head in fake sadness.

She rolled her eyes at him. "I did like you, Dimmy. I kind of still do. I mean, you don't get over someone in a week's time. Putting our friendship in jeopardy was not worth it. You're my best friend, Dimmy, and it sucks arse that we don't talk anymore. And when we do talk, we ignore all the things that drove us apart."

This time she spoke the truth. Not a single lie was uttered this evening and in all honesty, she felt that she deserved a pat on the back for that. She wasn't lying to anyone. But she was still lying to herself about the letter that still lay on the kitchen counter, beneath the other piles of letters that her parents had received.

"I wish I hadn't kissed you. I wish that we could go back in time to kindergarten when we first became friends, when everything was nice, peaceful, happy and not chaotic... A time when everything made sense."

Silence had settled upon them. Juniper's ragged breaths as she tried to recover from her little rant, as well as the hustle and bustle of the evening, was all that could be heard.

Then Dimitri broke the silence, his gaze turning warm and caring. "We can," he said.

"We can?" she asked slightly confused.

"It's called starting over, June. Do you not watch those sappy chick flicks or cheesy movies?" Dimitri asked with a small smile on his lips.

Juniper smirked. "No, but I know someone who does," she winked at him.

Dimitri rolled his eyes at her. "That's not the point. The point is that you and I are a lot alike. We both want things we can't exactly have yet we try to get it and in the end, we destroy. So how about we put the past behind us. I would say forgive and forget but going to jail is not something that I can easily forget." He smiled. "We can both forgive and move on."

Juniper smiled. She liked the sound of that. "Forgive and move on, huh? How?"

Dimitri's lips tilted up, half amused by the situation. Then he held out his hand. "Hi there," he said, "I'm Dimitri Remirez. My dad's half Italian and my Mum is British." He chuckled as he awaited Juniper's response.

That's how Dimitri introduced himself in kindergarten. Juniper remembered that this was almost the same introduction he gave her when they met in kindergarten. So she slid her hand into his and gave it a firm shake, just like she had in kindergarten, and decided that she should make the same introduction.

"Hello. My name is Juniper Stauff but please do call me June. I'm a native American, though I can imitate a British accent and can totally pass as a Brit. And I'd like to be your best friend."

Except this didn't change the fact Dimitri's and Juniper's friendship wasn't ever going to be the same. Even though Juniper had gotten all the forgiveness that she sought out, from Charlie, Amanda and Dimitri, nothing was going to remain as it once had been. Charlie still kept an eye on Juniper because now his brother had taken an interest in her. Amanda was always cautious around Juniper, making sure not to smile too much and analysing Juniper when she wasn't looking. Dimitri was probably the sincerest of the three but still their friendship wasn't ever going to be the same.

Juniper couldn't mend the things she had broken.

She was no superhero.

Chapter 18

Seated in Connor's Corner, a café Juniper Stauff had grown to love over the years, she was bored out of her mind. She had a date with Jeremy Cox. It wasn't actually a date. Jeremy wanted to hang out with Juniper but Juniper liked to think that it was a date.

He was running late. Half and hour late. With nothing better to do than just sip at her tea she averted her gaze outside the big window and watched the people pass by. It was half an hour past five and the streets were busy; cars moving to and fro, people walking in a rush so they could reach the safety and comfort of their homes to relax in after a day's long worth of work.

While waiting for Jeremy, Juniper decided to occupy her mind with university choices. She had always wanted to study Chemistry and with graduation soon approaching she found it fitting to go university hunting. All she knew was that most of her classmates intended to go to the University of Sereneigo and while it was quite a prestigious university filled with every course a student would desire to take, she wanted to be far away from all of this. She wanted to start over. She wanted another shot at life. Starting over in a completely new place, surrounded by completely new people, seemed like the perfect opportunity and Juniper had to take a hold of it before it slipped right through her fingers.

A hand tapped her shoulder and her head shot up as she was pulled out of her reverie. A smile took over her pink lips as she looked at the man that stood before her. His blonde hair was stuck in a red cap and, some of his hair spilling out over his ears and at the base of his neck. He had on plain black jeans which he had paired with an odd shirt. It had the words Pizzeria Kingdom written across it - sort of like what the waiters and waitresses at Pizzeria Kingdom wore.

He slid into the seat opposite of hers, his smile matching hers as his eyes held an apologetic look. "I'm so sorry I'm late. I forgot to tell you that I have work," he said sounding out of breath, "I actually ran most of the way. Well, walked but walking is so much exercise."

A soft chuckle left Juniper's lips. His words had managed to put a smile on her face. It took a little to no convincing to get Jeremy's number from Charlie. Charlie didn't mind that his brother and the girl that wasn't on his most liked list at that moment were hanging out. In fact, it made him happy that his brother had found someone to bond with with and he did not care if that person was one that he liked or not. All he cared for was his brother's happiness - he always had cared.

"I didn't know you started working," Juniper said.

"I was actually filling in for someone about a week ago for old times sake and apparently they missed my charm because it brought more customers, never mind the fact that they had always been mostly girls. So I'm rehired now." The smile on his lips radiated warmth and happiness and Juniper was filled with a sudden glow. It pleased her to see Jeremy like this. She was not quite over his drastic change. He was much nicer, kinder and quite different. However, Juniper knew that he didn't entirely change. His dark character was hidden beneath the fake smiles and Juniper saw it shimmer on the surface.

"That's great!" she beamed. "I'm glad you found something to occupy yourself. Have you thought of studying again?"

"I actually have. Journalism has always been a dream of mine so even though I'm twenty-two in a few months I'm looking for universities. I don't have much money now but I'm hoping to work my arse off this year. I'm looking for universities and which I should apply to in the meantime."

"Me too!" she exclaimed, the news making her excited. She hadn't talked to many people in her class about university. And if she did they all seemed fixated on the University of Sereneigo and how was she to talk about universities when the university they all wanted to attend was one that was on the very bottom of her choices. "Do you have any universities in mind?" she asked eagerly.

Jeremy chuckled at her curiousness. He was hesitant to tell Juniper a part of the truth but he decided that he had nothing to hide after he came out of rehab. Most people saw the brightness in Juniper and Jeremy had managed to spot out the flaws. He saw the inkling of darkness that tainted her soul. He could see her insecurities as if they were laid out right in front of him.

No, Juniper wasn't an open book but only a few people were able to see Juniper's true colours at first glance. There was something about her that drew Jeremy towards her. He was unable to place a finger on what exactly it was but there was question marks all around her. He wanted to know more about her but was she willing enough to open up to him?

"Any university that isn't in Sereneigo," he replied after a short pause. Some part of him hoped that she wouldn't ask why but the bigger part of him yearned for her to ask. He was alone for three years and all he wanted was company that could care for him.

Juniper looked at him and for a second Jeremy was unable to tell what was going on in Juniper's mind. Then her expression turned into one of that of happiness. "I swear I thought I was the only one who didn't want to go to the University of Sereneigo."

This didn't take him by surprise. "I'm guessing you want to leave her for a reason, too." The words slipped out of his mouth harshly and for a second his old self showed before a smile was back on his lips and he tilted his head in curiosity.

She had frozen, her eyes losing the vibrant colour as she looked at him. Her expression changed and there was the flawful Juniper seated opposite him. She was insecure, vulnerable and scared. And to cover this all up she pretended to be someone she really wasn't. A half of her was true while the other half of her seemed to be fake; all lies. He didn't know how long it was going to take for her to realise that she should stop trying to impress other people and do things for herself.

"How did you know?" she asked, her voice was low and accusing.

A smile crept its way to his lips as he laid his hands down on the table. "Once upon a time there was girl who thought herself to be a superhero. And she was one. She tried to bring peace as well as joy and happiness into the world. She solved disputes. What made her different from any other superhero was that she was never violent. Until one day she cracked. Being nice didn't always have its perks. She thought being nice would earn her a lot of things, that it would give her what she wanted.

"She wanted a heart but that heart belonged to someone else and that was the day that the superhero went rogue. She realised her mistakes a little too late - after all the damage had been made and blood had been split.

"The only solution that was left was to move away from the chaos and havoc and start afresh - be a better superhero because she learned from her mistakes."

Juniper sat silently across Jeremy, her mouth agape and shock shone clearly in her eyes. Under the table Jeremy had crossed his fingers. It dawned Juniper that Charlie must have told him about the deal that went on between Juniper and Charlie.

Her eyes turned cold and she fisted her hands, bringing them to the tabletop and staring at the man across her, accusingly. "Who are you?" Juniper asked, mixed emotions running through her eyes. Hurt, sadness and anger. Jeremy knew that some of the emotions she felt was directed at him but most of the emotions she felt was directed at the rawness of the truth he uttered.

"Who do you think you are?" Juniper questioned. It surprised Jeremy a little to see her flip in such a short time being in his presence. He wasn't expecting this reaction.

"I'm Jeremy Cox-"

"You can't come waltzing into my life-"

"Actually it was the other way around if you remember-"

"And you claim to know me but we've only met a few times-"

"Juniper!" Jeremy exclaimed taking a hold of her fist before she did anything drastic with them. Customers were already giving them the weird eye, some concerned while others were mildly amused as they thought that this was some sort of break up - only, Juniper and Jeremy weren't exactly a couple.

"Remember when I got out of the hospital? You said you wanted to save me, that you wanted to be a superhero," he said, his eyes holding cautious yet caring look that was putting Juniper slowly at ease. "I don't know much about superheroes but what I do know is that they do not run away from their fears. The fact that makes them a super hero is that they own up to their fear and face them. They don't let fear dominate their minds."

Her lips trembled, her blue eyes outlined with tears. "I did face my fears. I stood up to them. But see, life is a funny thing. It likes to throw that all back at your face. I just - I want everything to go back to the way it was before all this drama entered my life. And I know it was my fault and that I brought this upon myself but I... I just want things to be the same and go back to the way they once were. Why is that so damn hard?" She looked at him like he held all the answers. And maybe he did. Maybe he was her answer.

He squeezed her hands, a small smile gracing his face and adorning his captivative features. "Change, my dear superhero, is inevitable. It cannot be stopped. In certain situations it's considered as a bad thing while in other situations it's considered as a good thing. No matter how much you deny it, the little stunt you pulled changed your life and others as well. It's your perspective so it's up to you to tell if that change is for the better or for the worse."

She looked at him closely and this time she was the one giving Jeremy the analytic-calculating look. She was trying to decode him, trying to read him like he read her. But it was to no avail for she could not see anything she did not already know. He was a good actor, she'll give him that.

"Aren't you mad at me?" she finally asked as she broke the silence.

He released her hands and leaned back on his seat, his face holding a care-free expression. "Am I supposed to be mad at you?" he asked.

"You're telling me that you're not the least bit angry with me because I hurt your younger brother?" Juniper was confused. Why couldn't he just act like a normal human being and stop frustrating her?

"What you did to my brother did make me angry. Nobody hurts Charlie. It takes more than a bulldozer to hurt him so what you did must have been pretty hurtful. But I'm more disappointed. Juniper, you out of all people should not have gone along with that friend of yours. What's his name? Daniel? Dave? Dean?-"

"Dimitri," she corrected but her voice was small. He was right. If her parents were to find out about her failed schemes they would not only be disappointed in their daughter but in themselves as well. Mr and Mrs Stauff had always been anxious in raising a kid and hoped that whatever they did for Juniper was good enough, that they would raise her right.

"You're right," she said at last as she voiced her thoughts. "I'm a superhero and I wanted the one thing that I couldn't have; forbidden love. So I did horrible things to get it. I put friendship in jeopardy, I went against my word and even then true love was an obstacle that I couldn't overcome. I'm not really a superhero, am I?" Right then she didn't feel like a teenager. She felt old and weak.

Jeremy simply smiled and for some reason she felt that smile calm her nerves down. She was unable to understand why around him, one moment she was all riled up and then the next moment she was calm. His effect on her dazed and confused her and she was curious as to why she was acting this way - a way she hadn't acted before.

"You're a different kind of superhero then." He shrugged, a small smile gracing his lips. "Also, this conversation has me dying for a cigarette. How about we head for some pizza at Pizzeria Kingdom? I could even be your personal waiter," he said, adding the last bit with a flirtatious wink.

While Juniper disapproved of his smoking habits she couldn't help but giggle at his words. "I'm craving pizza," she replied.

"I'll take that as a yes," he said as he slid out of the booth, his eyes crinkling in the corners as he smiled. He looked very handsome when he smiled like that and it made Juniper's heart do a double take.

They exited the cafe, the ringing of the bell against the door as they departed sounded off softly in their ears. Once they were out Jeremy pulled out a pack and then a cigarette. Pulling out a lighter and lighting the cigarette, he took a long drag before he let out a huff of breath. Stuffing the lighter into his pockets, he faced Juniper and offered it to her. She shook her head, the stale smell already making her feel sick. "I don't smoke," she said. It could make my condition worse and I don't want that, she thought to herself.

Suddenly she needed a distraction. She needed to think of anything but her sickness. "What's your favourite season?" she asked, her abrupt question taking Jeremy by surprise.

"Oh," he chuckled. "I'll have to say spring because everything starts a new. Quite beautiful too. Why do you ask?"

"Just curious," she replied with a shrug of her shoulders. "I've always loved autumn. I don't see the falling leaves as a bad thing. I like to see it as shedding off the bad; a chance to actually live before you die."

"I never knew you could be so deep," he said as he took another drag of his cigarette. The pace they were walking at slowed as they both felt more comfortable in each other's presence.

"That's quite surprising since you claim to know everything about me," Juniper said, a little sarcasm dripping into her cheerful tone.

His gaze met hers and he couldn't help but smile and feel amused by her unusual antics. "You and I are quite alike, Juniper Stauff."

His words confused her. Were they supposed to compliment her or offend her? Since she didn't know what was implied by his statement, she voiced her thoughts. "How so?"

He had come to a complete standstill, holding Juniper's elbow to bring her to a halt. He dropped his cigarette to the floor and put his foot on top of it. She looked at him, her curious gaze growing only more curious as the noise of rush hour filled the silence.

"How are we alike? Well, that's a pretty good question," Jeremy replied. "We both like to put up façades to cover up who we truly are."

"You just admitted to me that you're wearing a façade."

"And you didn't deny that you're wearing one, too."

She smiled. "Touché."

He returned the smile. "Think about it this way: you and I are surrounded by deteriorating hearts. We all have something to lose. For me it was my father. For you it was your wild, dreamland fantasies. For Charlie it was his reputation. For my mother it was her grandparents, my great grandparents who had died at war. Do you see, Juniper? Of course all of us are not identical to each other but we all have lost something. We all have a reason to stop doing, to stop breathing, to stop living. Simultaneously, we all have a reason to do, to breathe, to live. This is how every individual is alike to each other. It's because of their hearts. Put together hearts have power. However, if hearts were torn apart they would disintegrate into nothingness as they await for darkness to swallow them whole. We have hearts but because of the trauma's of life we have endured, it is no more whole. A small bite has been taken out of our hearts and slowly our hearts deteriorate. You're not the only one with a deteriorating heart, June. Every individual has their own terrifying story and every individual has their own deteriorating heart."

By the time Jeremy was finished, his breath came out haggard, his face brighter than Juniper had ever seen. Her own deteriorating heart beat wildly within the confinements of her chest, his words slowly sinking into her as she absorbed them and kept them locked up in her mind, saving that silent promise.

Her face had changed to hopeful and she had never looked truer than she did right then. She was not pretending, she was not silencing her vulnerability. No, she was opening, blossoming for the lack of the better word, into a new person; into who she truly was.

"I'm not alone," she said softly almost like a delicate whisper. She meant what she said as a statement but once she uttered those words, it sounded as more of a question than a statement.

"Of course you're not," Jeremy said as his hand found hers and he squeezed her fingers, putting all his ounce of certainty into that caring squeeze.

Her warm smile matched his before she bumped his shoulder against hers, teasingly. "All this deep talk really has me hungry now," she quipped, her words making Jeremy laugh in amusement.

"C'mon," he said, tugging at her hand.

With Juniper's hand perfectly fitting in his, they walked to Pizzeria Kingdom. The weight that Juniper had bore for so long was finally lifted off her shoulders as a sense of relief and freedom entered her.

Now that everything was settled everyone presumed that life was rainbows and sunshine for Juniper Stauff. That day when Jeremy said she had a deteriorating heart - that she already knew. He said that every person had their own deteriorating heart but what made her deteriorating heart different from most people was that fact that in Juniper's case, her deteriorating heart was literal.

And that ladies and gentlemen is the truth about Juniper Stauff that had always been tucked into the confinements of a small envelope that laid on her kitchen table. No one but her parents and Dimitri knew that she had breast cancer. She was still in her early stages and she hated the sound of treatment. That was the secret she had buried so deep that often she forgot about her condition. She wanted to act wild and spontaneous, to take advantage of life while it was still there for her.

And moving away, onto another battlefield and playing the role of a better superhero, she will face the death that she truly deserved; one filled with peace, serenity and most of all, content.

Literal or not, the moment her life turned upside down - which includes being diagnosed with breast cancer - Juniper Stauff knew that she had a broken, unfixable, deteriorating heart.

EPILOGUE

It is said that people move away because they are running away from their fears and insecurities. This description did not exactly fit Juniper Stauff's situation. Juniper was moving away to get a fresh start, to be a new superhero and to die a heroic death.

Juniper Stauff had come to terms with her sudden shortened life span. Before the chaos that she had unleashed into her world, she was just a normal girl trying to blend in by being someone she truly wasn't entirely and get through high school which was the aim of every teenager that was to ever walk the corridors of Phantom High.

Occasionally Mr and Mrs Stauff would force Juniper to go for check ups. Being doctors themselves they put health as one of their top priorities. If Juniper was as enthusiastic about health as her parents were then she would have visited the doctor more regularly and she would have taken the treatment for her condition.

When Juniper did oblige to her parents wishes and went for a check up because her parents had seen the slight symptoms and as doctors, they were immediately consumed with worry -

that was when everything went downhill. That was the day that Juniper had learnt that she was suffering from breast cancer. That was the day the superhero decided to rebel and claim what was not rightfully hers. She did horrible things and caused havoc. She caused a strain in the loyalty that she had gained. She caused a hole in a lovely friendship and she back-stabbed her best friend. All to attain something that was never attainable in the first place; a broken heart that throbbed for someone else and not her.

She was a hero and what sort of an example was she setting, as a hero, if she unleashed chaos? But she was also human as well and being human, she was bound to mess up at one point and make mistakes. She was bound to surrender to desire.

The boarding to her flight was about to commence in half an hour and she decided now was the perfect time to bid farewell to all those who cared enough to say goodbye which was her parents and Dimitri only.

"Amanda couldn't make it," Dimitri said. "She needed to go out with her mum somewhere. I didn't really ask."

Juniper nodded, her heart sinking at the news. Juniper knew Dimitri was lying and that Amanda was still not comfortable with Juniper. Things weren't exactly the same between them and Juniper was glad to be leaving this place. She wouldn't be bothering anyone anymore.

"She did tell me to tell you that she ships you and Jeremy though," Dimitri teased, wiggling his brows. Juniper blinked twice before smacking Dimitri's shoulder.

She giggled slightly at Dimitri's proclamation but then turned her head so she could get a glimpse of Jeremy. He stood with his mother and Charlie and they were talking very animatedly.

His mother bore a happy expression even though tears simmered at the brim of her eyes while Jeremy had an arm slung around Charlie, telling him something with a goofy smile on his lips. Charlie nodded but not before he gave Jeremy the famous Charlie eye roll.

Juniper and Jeremy both decided to move to a new place together. Jeremy had a university fund that his mother had kept for him even after he went to rehab in case he wanted to change his life. And he did want to change his life. With someone new; with Juniper. They were both going to attend the same university and share an apartment together. So, in a way, Dimitri was right. Feelings between them were not going to stay platonic forever, especially when Jeremy seemed to read Juniper so much more easily than most people could.

She turned back to Dimitri to see a knowing smirk slung over his lisp. "What?" she asked defensively.

"I think my ship may be sailing," Dimitri winked.

"Oh, shut up," Juniper blushed as she pushed her shoulder against his. "Wait, I thought you said Amanda shipped Jeremy and I?"

Dimitri chuckled, holding his hands in the air. "Caught red-handed."

Juniper laughed at his reply. "There might be a ship. Who knows?"

He smiled slyly at her before his smile dimmed and his eyes held another look to it - sadness. He opened his arms as he took a step forward and Juniper ducked her head beneath his, tucking it in place before wrapping her arms around his waist and drawing her best friend - that was what he was to her once upon a time - closer to herself. She knew what was best for her heart. Her heart told her that she had to move on. She's been telling herself that the past few weeks and while her feelings were not as prominent as the night she kissed Dimitri, they still had not disappeared. First love was always tough.

"Remember when you wanted a unicorn for your fifth birthday?" Dimitri asked, his hand rubbing slow circles on her back, like he had always done. Juniper sunk further into his embrace the more he spoke. "And when you wanted to go to Hogwarts after you watched a marathon of all the Harry Potter movies? Oh, and there was that time when you heard OneRepublic was coming to town but that turned out to be just a rumour and you cried. Oh my, remember that time when you were fourteen and you fell when you attempted to climb a tree? I was there to heal your wounds."

Juniper felt Dimitri shaking. He didn't want to let go but he had to. He pulled back, his soft brown eyes glassy. He sniffed. "Then there were those times when I wished people would look at me the way you do." A haunting look took over his adorable features and the emotion of guilt washed over his expression. "Time changed us both and now... Now I feel different. I feel like there's something about you that I just still can't figure out. I wanted to be your best friend. That's what we were supposed to be. What happened to us, June?"

A lump had grown in her throat and tears appeared in her eyes. "Time, Dimmy. It changed us and what we were supposed to be." She did not want to admit that her selfish reasons had caused the strain in their friendship. No, she was past that and she was no longer going to hold onto the past by constantly blaming herself. What's done was done. There was nothing that she could do to change that fact.

"It's not the same any more, is it?"

She nodded because for once, Juniper didn't have a reply for her best friend. Then she looked into his brown eyes, the ones she once fell in love with, and said, "will you miss me, Dimmy?"

"Is that even a question?" he smiled lightly.

She chuckled. "But will you?"

"Of course, I would." Then a moment of silence passed by as both Juniper and Dimitri soaked in everything. "Will you miss me, June?"

"Every freaking day," she replied before giving him one last tight hug. He was right. Time had changed them and transformed them into people that neither of them recognised.

"Have a safe flight," he said and leaned down, pressing his lips to her cheek for old times sake. The kiss now seemed different and wrong while before all this chaos, it would be innocent. But she smiled nonetheless because at least he was attempting to do something that was always done when they parted. Except this time they were parting forever and that brief kiss spoke in volumes.

He waved her goodbye and she watched his retreating figure before her parents jumped into her line of vision. "What, so now only Dimitri gets to say goodbye?" Mrs Stauff said teasingly.

Juniper laughed before she turned her full attention to her parents, her eyes watering at the sight of them. Her father's eyes held pride while her mother's lips trembled. She pulled her parents into a bear hug and let their arms drape over her protectively.

"You will try to visit, won't you?" her mother croaked, her voice wavering.

"Of course I'll try, mama," Juniper replied, her throat swelling up as she did her best to hold down the sob.

"And you will do your best and make us proud, won't you?" her father asked, his eyes glassy.

"My very best, papa," Juniper replied.

When she saw both their content smiles, that's when she broke down.

"No, no, no," her mother cooed, smoothing down Juniper's hair. "There's no need to cry. Mama and Papa will always be here for you."

"Forever and always, baby girl," Mr Stauff said, taking Juniper back into his strong arms. He held onto his daughter, afraid of what the outside world had to offer to his little princess.

"Are you sure you want to go?" asked Mr Stauff. He wanted his daughter to study here; close to her parents. But she was insistent on moving out and living somewhere else. He knew part of the reason as to why she was so insistent but he was not ready to let go of his daughter, especially because she refused treatment and the world could swallow her up at any second.

Mr and Mrs Stauff were not afraid nor anxious for their daughter's fate but they were saddened - especially Mr Stauff - by the fact that his daughter would not die in his hands but in a foreign place, far away from him.

"Papa," Juniper said, her eyes watering at his statement. He gathered her into his arms once more, not quite sure if this was the last time he was going to see her or when she was able to come back and visit them. The uncertainty of the whole situation really got to him. When he released her, he looked away as he blinked rapidly. He did not want Juniper to witness him tearing up.

Mrs Stauff cupped Juniper's face, tears running down both their faces when a voice filled the airport informing them that there were only a few minutes till boarding was due to start.

At the sound of the monotonous voice that filled the airport, Mrs Stauff hugged her daughter with all her might. "Be a good child, June," her mother whispered to her. Then she held her daughter away at arm's length. "Don't give up on that lovely dream of yours. Be a superhero, June. Be your mama's superhero."

Tears gathered once more in Juniper's eyes and she hugged her parents one last time, a longing feeling had already settled within her. She was going to miss them. She was going to miss this. She was going to miss everything.

She bid her parents farewell, wiping her face with the back of her sleeve as she put on a strong smile. Once she arrived at where the Cox's family were standing at, she hugged Mrs Cox, promising her that she will look after Jeremy. Then she turned to Charlie who hugged her as well, who whispered threateningly into her ear, "hurt my brother and I'll kill you. He seems more interested in you now so please do me a favour, June, and make my brother a happy man."

She pulled back, an amusing smile dangling on her lips. "I'll try my best, Charles."

"Don't call me that," he instantly bit out, and then hesitantly added, "thanks."

Both Jeremy and Juniper then walked away from their families, not once glancing back in fear that they may cower away from this opportunity and run back into their beloved families arms.

Jeremy slipped his hand into Juniper's and gave it a slight squeeze as they stood in line. "Ready?" he smiled.

She took a deep breath before she replied. "Ready."

Jeremy's head lolled over and rested on Juniper's shoulder due to exhaustion at some part of the journey. They were both tired and worn out but Juniper could not bring herself to fall asleep no matter how heavy her lids grew.

She sat there, with Jeremy's head resting against her shoulder, and simply thought and thought and thought until all she was doing was thinking. What did her future hold for her? Was Jeremy going to be a constant in her future? She did not expect to live long nor did she expect a long future but she wanted to make everything out of nothing. She wanted a future - even if said future was to be short lived.

She was leaving Dimitri, her parents and chaos behind. It was in that moment, as she sat quietly thinking to herself, that she replayed the the conversation that Dimitri and her shared at the airport. She was going to miss him. She was never going to forget him. Moving on didn't necessarily mean forgetting the one whom you first loved, did it? All Juniper knew was that she had to move on. One step backwards, two steps forward.

The pilot's voice filled the plane announcing that they were due to land soon and that was what brought Juniper out of her deep reverie. Juniper shook Jeremy's side slightly, lifting his head up in the process of waking him up from his light slumber.

"Mhm?" he groaned sleepily, lifting his head fully up so he could peer at Juniper. His sandy blonde hair stuck out in odd angles and Juniper could not help but smile at how boyish and cute he looked like that with bed-head. She'd be getting to see this attractive appearance every morning soon enough and a slight blush crept up her neck at the mere thought of sharing an apartment with Jeremy.

"Put your seatbelt on," Juniper instructed, smiling. "We're about to land."

He nodded groggily, still recovering from sleep. After fastening his seatbelt he held out his hand and Juniper smiled at him after she clasped his outstretched hand and gave it an a tight squeeze. This was the first time that Jeremy was going on a plane - that Mr and Mrs Stauff had insisted on paying for - and the take off had frightened him out of his wits. He had closed his eyes and began shaking, barring his hands into fists and repetitively whispering under his breath, "you will not die, you will not die, you will not die."

Juniper had immediately reached over and laid her hand on top of his, easing out his fist and slipping her hands through his so as to intertwine their fingers together. "Breathe, Jeremy," Juniper had said, rubbing slow circled at the back of his hand with her thumb. It was hard but once they were in the air, Jeremy had calmed down and loosened his grip on Juniper's hand who in return, clutched at his hand tighter, shaking her head. "I like holding your hand," she blatantly stated before she turned her attention to the small television screen that was behind the front person's seat. She hadn't miss the way his enticing lips had lifted up into a satisfied smile.

Now, clasping Juniper's hand upon landing, with no words exchanged, he seemed much more calmer than he was at take off. Juniper gave his hand an encouraging squeeze to which he squeezed her hand back. Juniper smiled and let out a content sigh as she closed her eyes and prepared for the landing of the plane.

Soon both Juniper and Jeremy were out of the confinements of the aeroplane and the airport, and were thrust into their new home. Juniper breathed in the scent of a fresh start, her hand not once leaving Jeremy's. This was her second chance. This was Jeremy's second chance. In fact, this was their second chance. She had not felt more joy as she had did right then.

Juniper Stauff was going to make the most of her life and live her life to the fullest, however long her deteriorating heart permitted her to do just as she desired.